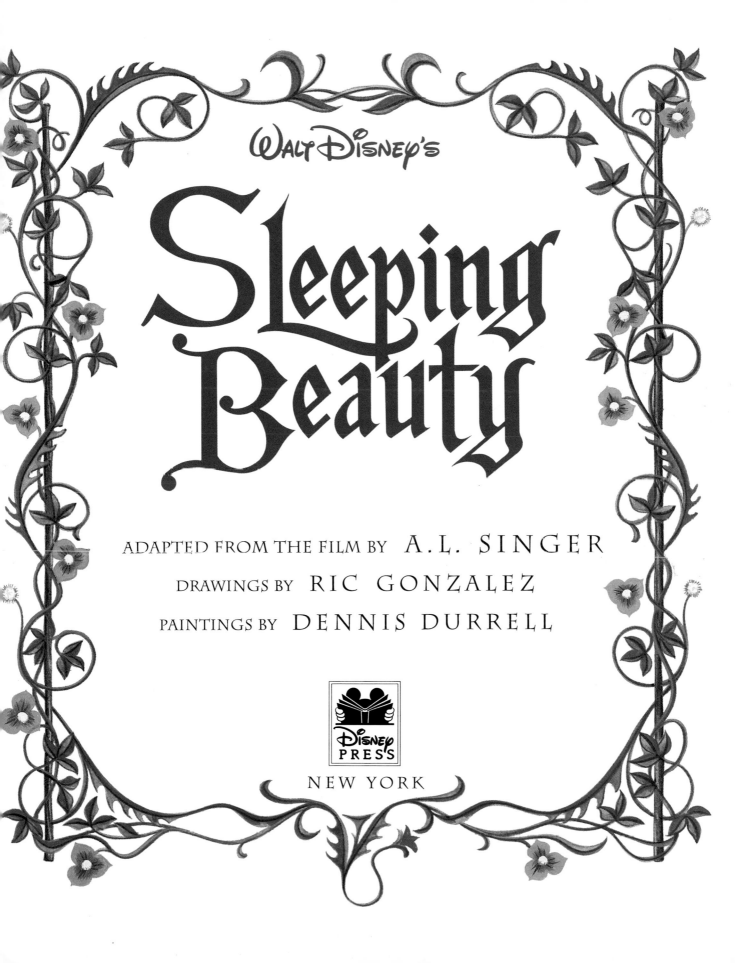

Walt Disney's

Sleeping Beauty

ADAPTED FROM THE FILM BY A.L. SINGER

DRAWINGS BY RIC GONZALEZ

PAINTINGS BY DENNIS DURRELL

Disney
PRESS

NEW YORK

First Edition
1 3 5 7 9 10 8 6 4 2

Library of Congress Catalog Card Number: 92-56158
ISBN 1-56282-366-3 / 1-56282-367-1 (lib. bdg.)

CHAPTER ONE

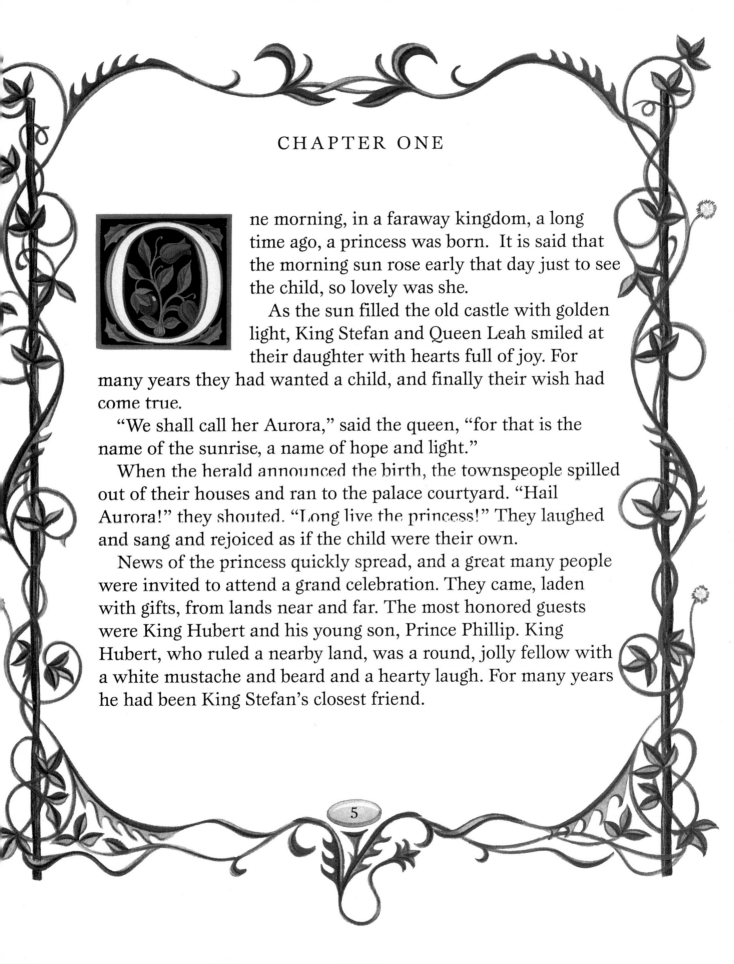

One morning, in a faraway kingdom, a long time ago, a princess was born. It is said that the morning sun rose early that day just to see the child, so lovely was she.

As the sun filled the old castle with golden light, King Stefan and Queen Leah smiled at their daughter with hearts full of joy. For many years they had wanted a child, and finally their wish had come true.

"We shall call her Aurora," said the queen, "for that is the name of the sunrise, a name of hope and light."

When the herald announced the birth, the townspeople spilled out of their houses and ran to the palace courtyard. "Hail Aurora!" they shouted. "Long live the princess!" They laughed and sang and rejoiced as if the child were their own.

News of the princess quickly spread, and a great many people were invited to attend a grand celebration. They came, laden with gifts, from lands near and far. The most honored guests were King Hubert and his young son, Prince Phillip. King Hubert, who ruled a nearby land, was a round, jolly fellow with a white mustache and beard and a hearty laugh. For many years he had been King Stefan's closest friend.

As Prince Phillip bowed to King Stefan, his blond hair fell over his eyes. The two kings chuckled and exchanged a warm glance. "Hubert, I have long dreamed that our kingdoms would unite into one," King Stefan said. "If my daughter marries your son, my dream will come to pass."

King Hubert's eyes lit up. "Then they *shall* marry," he said. "Let us decree it, Stefan!"

The two kings immediately told the herald to announce a royal proclamation of marriage. The herald quickly climbed the tower next to the courtyard and stepped to the window. The townspeople below grew silent.

"Hear ye! Hear ye!" the herald shouted. "Their Majesties King Stefan and King Hubert hereby announce the betrothal of Princess Aurora to Prince Phillip!"

A thunderous roar of happiness echoed through the throne room.

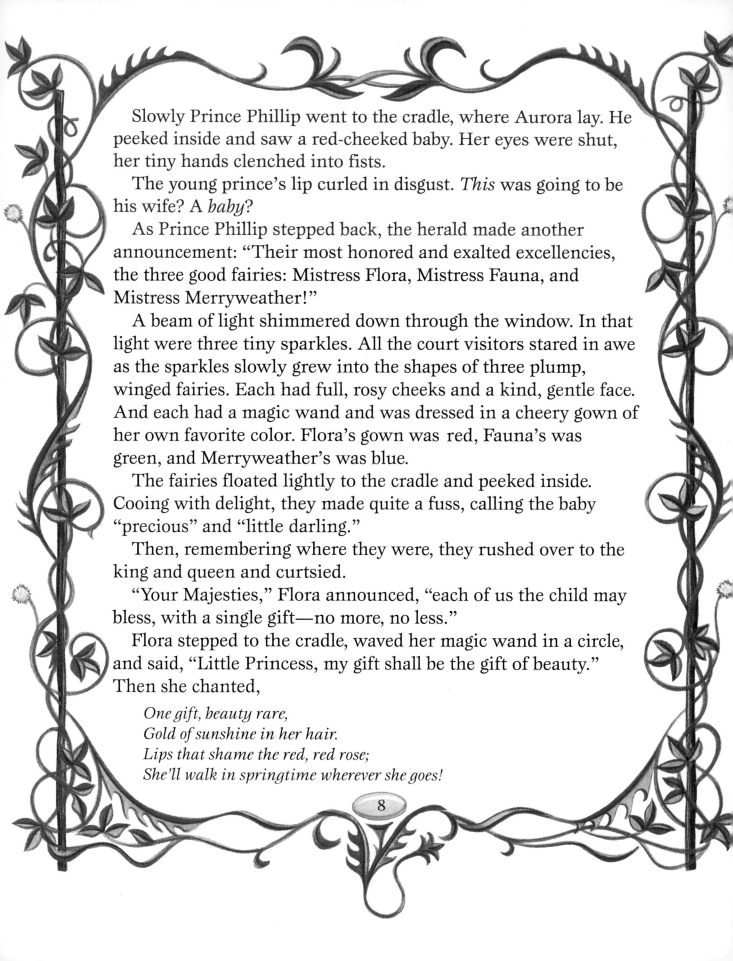

Slowly Prince Phillip went to the cradle, where Aurora lay. He peeked inside and saw a red-cheeked baby. Her eyes were shut, her tiny hands clenched into fists.

The young prince's lip curled in disgust. *This* was going to be his wife? A *baby*?

As Prince Phillip stepped back, the herald made another announcement: "Their most honored and exalted excellencies, the three good fairies: Mistress Flora, Mistress Fauna, and Mistress Merryweather!"

A beam of light shimmered down through the window. In that light were three tiny sparkles. All the court visitors stared in awe as the sparkles slowly grew into the shapes of three plump, winged fairies. Each had full, rosy cheeks and a kind, gentle face. And each had a magic wand and was dressed in a cheery gown of her own favorite color. Flora's gown was red, Fauna's was green, and Merryweather's was blue.

The fairies floated lightly to the cradle and peeked inside. Cooing with delight, they made quite a fuss, calling the baby "precious" and "little darling."

Then, remembering where they were, they rushed over to the king and queen and curtsied.

"Your Majesties," Flora announced, "each of us the child may bless, with a single gift—no more, no less."

Flora stepped to the cradle, waved her magic wand in a circle, and said, "Little Princess, my gift shall be the gift of beauty." Then she chanted,

> *One gift, beauty rare,*
> *Gold of sunshine in her hair.*
> *Lips that shame the red, red rose;*
> *She'll walk in springtime wherever she goes!*

Suddenly brightly colored sparkles swirled together high above the cradle. Spinning round and round, they transformed into beautiful flowers and fell gently around the baby princess.

Then Fauna stepped forward, waved her magic wand, and said,

Tiny Princess,
My gift shall be the gift of song;
Melody your whole life long!

A bright whirl of colors appeared again. Inside it, a magical image of a girl and a castle appeared. On the girl's finger was a nightingale, singing sweetly.

At last it was Merryweather's turn. She went to the cradle with her wand and said, "Sweet Princess, my gift shall be the—"
BOOOOOM!

A huge crash echoed through the throne room as the castle doors blew open with the fury of a tornado. Merryweather ran to the other fairies in fright. The king and queen stood up, their robes whipping around them. Banners snapped in the wind, and hats and helmets blew off of heads. With a sudden *crack* of thunder, the room grew dark.

Then a bolt of lightning struck the center of the room. Hissing green flames shot upward from the floor. Terrified, the townspeople backed away, gasping. A dark figure appeared in the flames—the figure of a tall, narrow woman shrouded in black. She held a long, thin staff with a glowing knob on top. An ugly black raven perched on the knob.

Her hard face was calm, but her eyes burned with fury. She stared around the court, finally fixing her gaze on the king.

"Why, it's Maleficent!" Fauna whispered to the other fairies.
"What does she want here?" Merryweather whispered back.
"Shhhhh!" Flora warned.

Maleficent's voice was smooth and low, but it was filled with coldness. "Well, quite a glittering assemblage, King Stefan," she said, looking around. "Royalty, nobility, the gentry, and ..."

She stopped a moment when she saw the three fairies. Her lips slowly curled into a sinister smile. "Oh, how quaint—you've even invited the rabble."

Merryweather's face scrunched with anger. "Ohhhh!" she cried, lunging forward.

Quickly Flora grabbed Merryweather's gown and pulled her back.

"I really felt quite distressed at not receiving an invitation," Maleficent continued.

"You weren't wanted!" Merryweather blurted.

"*Not want—?*" Maleficent began with a look of surprise, but she cut herself off. She began to pet her raven gently as if she hadn't a care in the world. "Oh dear, I had hoped it was due to some oversight. Well, in that event, I'd best be on my way."

With that, she turned to leave. The raven hopped off her staff and sat on her shoulder.

Queen Leah spoke up. "And you're not offended, Your Excellency?"

"Why, no, Your Majesty," Maleficent said, turning around. "And to show I bear no ill will, I, too, shall bestow a gift on the child."

The three fairies quickly crowded around the cradle, trying to protect the baby. They didn't believe for a minute that the evil witch was telling the truth.

Maleficent's face grew dark with hate. She brought her staff to the ground with a crash. "Listen well, all of you!" she bellowed. "The princess shall indeed grow in grace and beauty, beloved by all who know her. But before the sun sets on her sixteenth birthday, she shall prick her finger on the spindle of a spinning wheel and *die*!"

As she spoke, the small knob on top of her staff pulsed with light. It grew into a crystal ball, aglow with the image of a spinning wheel, its sharp spindle glistening. Bats flew around it, squealing and shrieking.

13

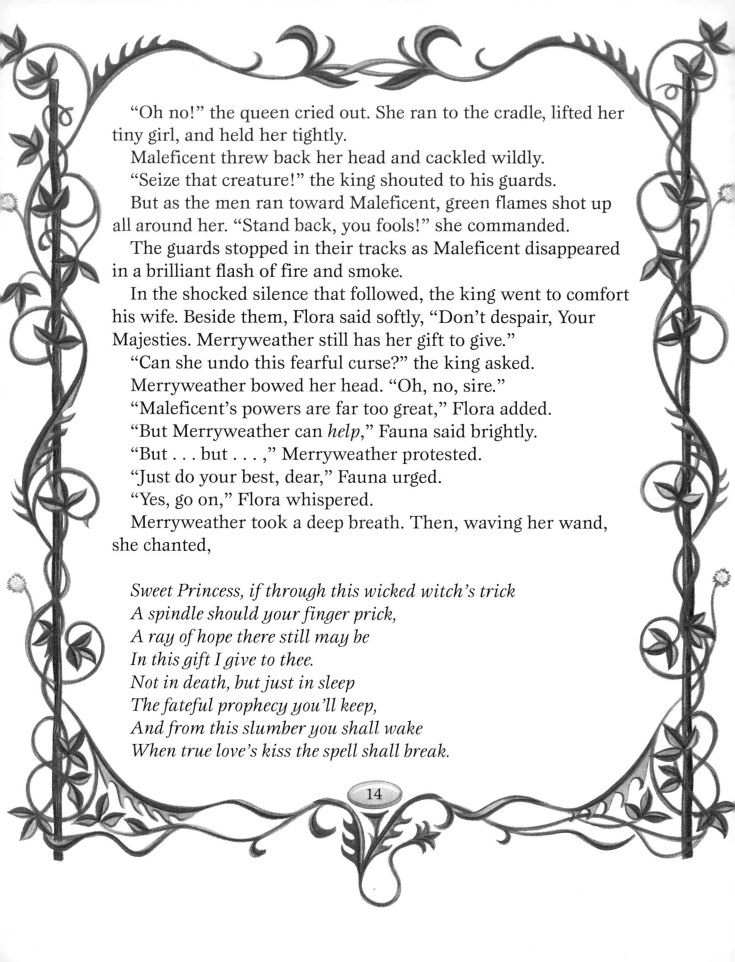

"Oh no!" the queen cried out. She ran to the cradle, lifted her tiny girl, and held her tightly.

Maleficent threw back her head and cackled wildly.

"Seize that creature!" the king shouted to his guards.

But as the men ran toward Maleficent, green flames shot up all around her. "Stand back, you fools!" she commanded.

The guards stopped in their tracks as Maleficent disappeared in a brilliant flash of fire and smoke.

In the shocked silence that followed, the king went to comfort his wife. Beside them, Flora said softly, "Don't despair, Your Majesties. Merryweather still has her gift to give."

"Can she undo this fearful curse?" the king asked.

Merryweather bowed her head. "Oh, no, sire."

"Maleficent's powers are far too great," Flora added.

"But Merryweather can *help*," Fauna said brightly.

"But . . . but . . . ," Merryweather protested.

"Just do your best, dear," Fauna urged.

"Yes, go on," Flora whispered.

Merryweather took a deep breath. Then, waving her wand, she chanted,

Sweet Princess, if through this wicked witch's trick
A spindle should your finger prick,
A ray of hope there still may be
In this gift I give to thee.
Not in death, but just in sleep
The fateful prophecy you'll keep,
And from this slumber you shall wake
When true love's kiss the spell shall break.

Would Merryweather's spell truly protect Aurora from death? King Stefan did not want to find out. He immediately gave an order for all the spinning wheels in the kingdom to be burned.

A fire soon blazed in the royal courtyard, fueled by spinning wheels new and old. But the king was still not satisfied. He had seen Maleficent's power. Perhaps she would simply create a spinning wheel by magic.

Something else had to be done to protect Aurora—but what?

he three fairies pondered this question for hours. They talked and talked, and talked some more. And after every last person had left the throne room, they were still talking.

Finally Flora heaved a great sigh and said, "Ohhhh, silly fiddle-faddle!"

Fauna sat down and waved her wand. Instantly a teapot appeared. Flora and Merryweather flopped down next to her. Halfheartedly they waved their wands and—*pop!* Three teacups were floating in the air.

"Well," Merryweather said between sips, "a bonfire won't stop Maleficent."

"Perhaps we can reason with her," Fauna said. "She can't be *all* bad."

Flora rolled her eyes. "Oh yes she can!"

"Ohhhh!" Merryweather said with frustration. "I'd like to turn her into a fat old hoptoad!"

"Now, dear, that isn't a very nice thing to say," Fauna said. "Besides, our magic can only do good—to bring joy and happiness."

Merryweather made a cookie appear and bit into it. "Well, turning her into a hoptoad would make *me* happy!" she grumbled.

"But there must be some way . . . ," Flora said. Suddenly her face lit up. "There is!"

"What is it, Flora?" Fauna asked.

"Shhh!" Fauna replied. "Even the walls have ears. Follow me!"

Zzzing! With a sweep of her wand, she made herself shrink to the size of a butterfly.

Zzzing! Zzzing! Flora and Merryweather did the same. They flew across the throne room, trailing sparkles like three tiny shooting stars.

On a table near the throne, there was a small decorative box. It was a gift for the baby princess, with a silver cup and spoon inside.

Flora, Fauna, and Merryweather flew inside and closed the box. Now no one would hear them. "I'll turn the princess into a flower!" Flora said, practically bursting with excitement. "A flower can't prick its finger, because it hasn't any! She'll be perfectly safe."

"Until Maleficent sends a frost," Merryweather remarked.

Flora's face sank. "Oh dear, you're right. And she'll be expecting us to do something like that."

"What *won't* she expect?" Merryweather said bitterly. "She knows everything."

"Oh, but she doesn't, dear," Fauna said. "Maleficent doesn't know anything about love or kindness or the joy of helping others."

Flora jumped up. "That's it! It's the only thing she can't understand, and she won't expect it!" She began pacing around, deep in thought. "Now, we'll have to plan. . . . Let's see, the abandoned woodcutter's cottage. . . . Of course, the king and queen will object, but when we explain it's the only way—"

"Explain what?" Merryweather interrupted.

"About the three peasant women raising a foundling child deep in the forest," Flora explained.

"Oh, that's very nice of them," Fauna said.

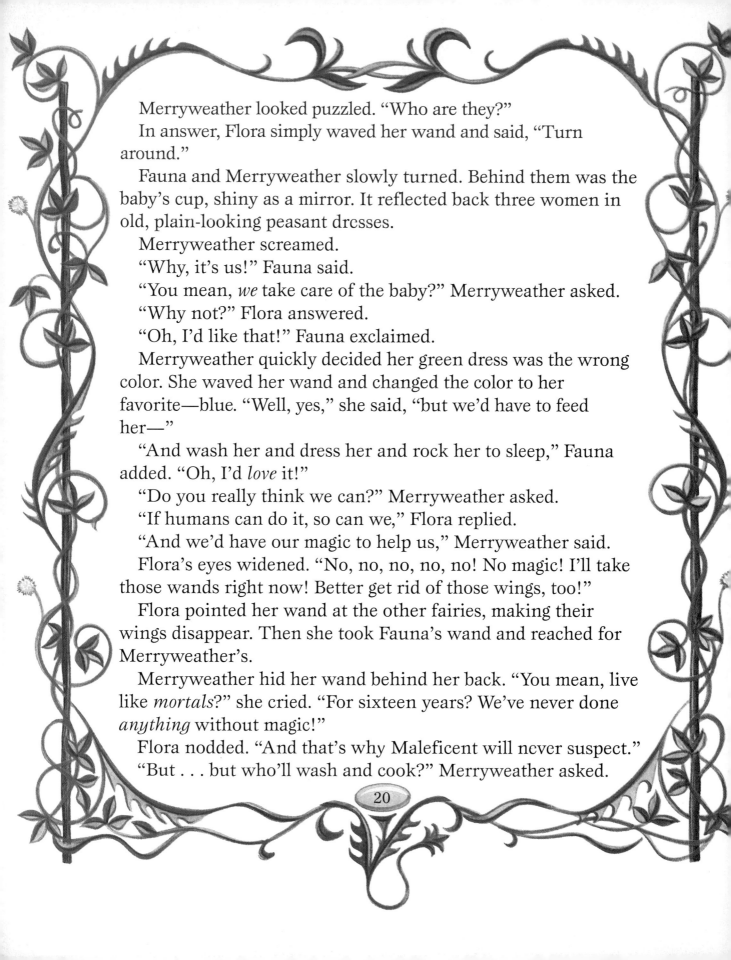

Merryweather looked puzzled. "Who are they?"

In answer, Flora simply waved her wand and said, "Turn around."

Fauna and Merryweather slowly turned. Behind them was the baby's cup, shiny as a mirror. It reflected back three women in old, plain-looking peasant dresses.

Merryweather screamed.

"Why, it's us!" Fauna said.

"You mean, *we* take care of the baby?" Merryweather asked.

"Why not?" Flora answered.

"Oh, I'd like that!" Fauna exclaimed.

Merryweather quickly decided her green dress was the wrong color. She waved her wand and changed the color to her favorite—blue. "Well, yes," she said, "but we'd have to feed her—"

"And wash her and dress her and rock her to sleep," Fauna added. "Oh, I'd *love* it!"

"Do you really think we can?" Merryweather asked.

"If humans can do it, so can we," Flora replied.

"And we'd have our magic to help us," Merryweather said.

Flora's eyes widened. "No, no, no, no, no! No magic! I'll take those wands right now! Better get rid of those wings, too!"

Flora pointed her wand at the other fairies, making their wings disappear. Then she took Fauna's wand and reached for Merryweather's.

Merryweather hid her wand behind her back. "You mean, live like *mortals*?" she cried. "For sixteen years? We've never done *anything* without magic!"

Flora nodded. "And that's why Maleficent will never suspect."

"But . . . but who'll wash and cook?" Merryweather asked.

"Oh, we'll all pitch in," Flora answered. She held out her hand. "Let's have the wand, dear."

With a sigh of frustration, Merryweather gave it to her.

Flora took all three wands in one hand. "Come along, now. We must tell Their Majesties at once."

Using Flora's magic, the fairies flew out of the box and grew back to their normal size. As they walked to the nursery, they chattered excitedly about how they would raise the princess.

But deep inside, none of them wanted to have to tell the king and queen. The plan was a good one, but it would surely break Their Majesties' hearts.

• • •

The fairies bravely explained their plan to the king and queen that afternoon. Then they left them alone to think. Later that night, the fairies entered the royal nursery. Dressed in their simple peasant garb, they humbly approached the king and queen. "Your Majesties . . . ?" Flora said. "Have you considered our plan?"

Queen Leah held out the sleeping baby princess, wrapped in thick, plain blankets. "Take good care of her," she said, her voice quivering. "And go quickly, before I change my mind."

Fauna gently took the baby and said, "We will see you at sunset on the princess's sixteenth birthday. Until then she will be in good hands."

The three fairies walked down the winding stairs of the castle tower. They would have to travel everywhere on foot now. The magic wands were hidden in Flora's dress, not to be touched for sixteen years.

The fairies hurried through the castle gate and into the countryside. Maleficent had spies everywhere, so they had to

travel quickly and quietly. Above them, the king and queen watched from a parapet. But the fairies made sure not to look back.

And it was a good thing, too, because the grief on Their Majesties' faces would have been enough to melt a heart of stone.

CHAPTER THREE

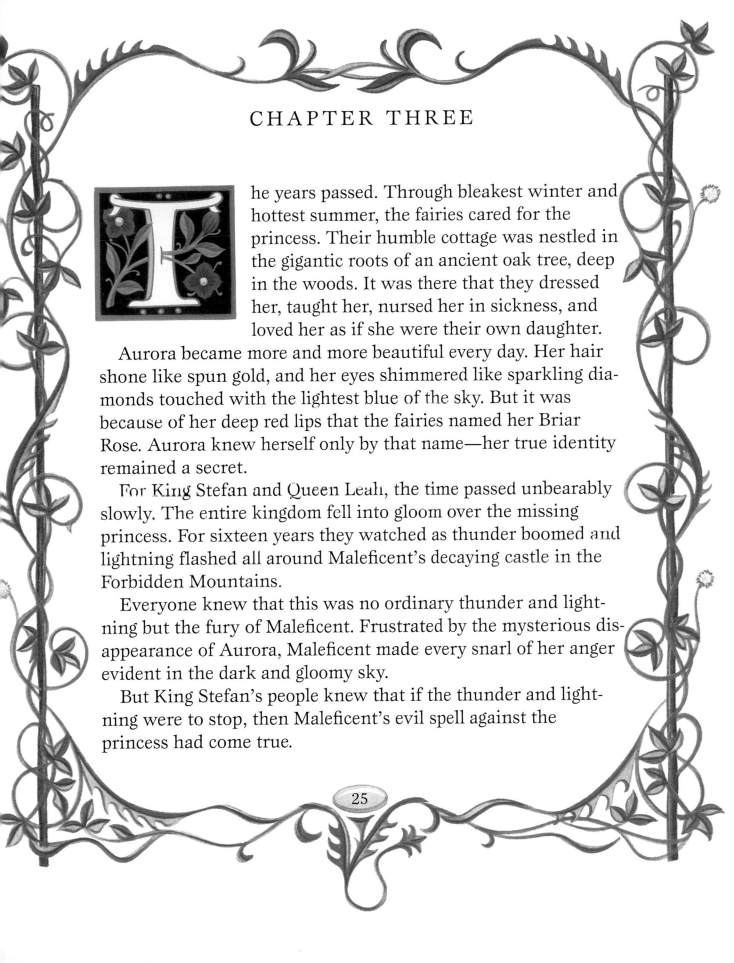

he years passed. Through bleakest winter and hottest summer, the fairies cared for the princess. Their humble cottage was nestled in the gigantic roots of an ancient oak tree, deep in the woods. It was there that they dressed her, taught her, nursed her in sickness, and loved her as if she were their own daughter.

Aurora became more and more beautiful every day. Her hair shone like spun gold, and her eyes shimmered like sparkling diamonds touched with the lightest blue of the sky. But it was because of her deep red lips that the fairies named her Briar Rose. Aurora knew herself only by that name—her true identity remained a secret.

For King Stefan and Queen Leah, the time passed unbearably slowly. The entire kingdom fell into gloom over the missing princess. For sixteen years they watched as thunder boomed and lightning flashed all around Maleficent's decaying castle in the Forbidden Mountains.

Everyone knew that this was no ordinary thunder and lightning but the fury of Maleficent. Frustrated by the mysterious disappearance of Aurora, Maleficent made every snarl of her anger evident in the dark and gloomy sky.

But King Stefan's people knew that if the thunder and lightning were to stop, then Maleficent's evil spell against the princess had come true.

On the eve of the princess's sixteenth birthday, the noisy storm was louder than ever. Finally the mood of the kingdom began to lift. Soon the princess's birthday would pass, and she would be home, safe.

• • •

Soon the princess's sixteenth birthday would pass. It was all Maleficent could think about, too. And it made her blood boil.

Her raven sat on her shoulders as she paced the crumbling floor of her throne room. She scowled angrily at a group of her warriors—all of them hideous, snout-faced monsters with sharp teeth and small brains. "It's incredible," she hissed. "Sixteen years and not a trace of her! Are you sure you searched everywhere?"

The warriors looked at each other dumbly. Finally the leader among them spoke up. "Uh . . . uh . . . yep, we looked everywhere! The town, uh, the mountains . . . uh, uh, the houses, and uh, let me see . . . uh, all the cradles!"

Maleficent stared at him. "Cradles?" she said, her eyes ablaze. "All these years you've been looking for a *baby*?"

She threw her head back and shrieked with laughter. One by one her warriors began to laugh, too.

"Idiots!" Maleficent shrieked. "Imbeciles!"

The warriors fell silent. Maleficent thrust her arm forward. With a deafening *zzzzzapp*, lightning bolts shot out from the tip of her staff.

"*Ooooo! Ooch! Ouch!* " Yelping with pain, the creatures jumped away from the lightning. They fell over each other trying to rush out the door.

Maleficent stormed over to her throne. Its cold stone seat was damp and cracked, its arms curving forward into sharp claws. "They're a disgrace to the forces of evil," she said to her raven.

"You are my last chance."

She lifted the raven in her hand and brought it to an open window. "Circle far and wide," she commanded. "Search for a maid of sixteen with hair of sunshine gold and lips red as the rose. Go, and do not fail me!"

With that, she released her beloved black-feathered pet. There wasn't much time; the girl's sixteenth birthday was the following day. But as Maleficent watched the raven fly into the thick clouds, she felt an evil glimmer of hope.

27

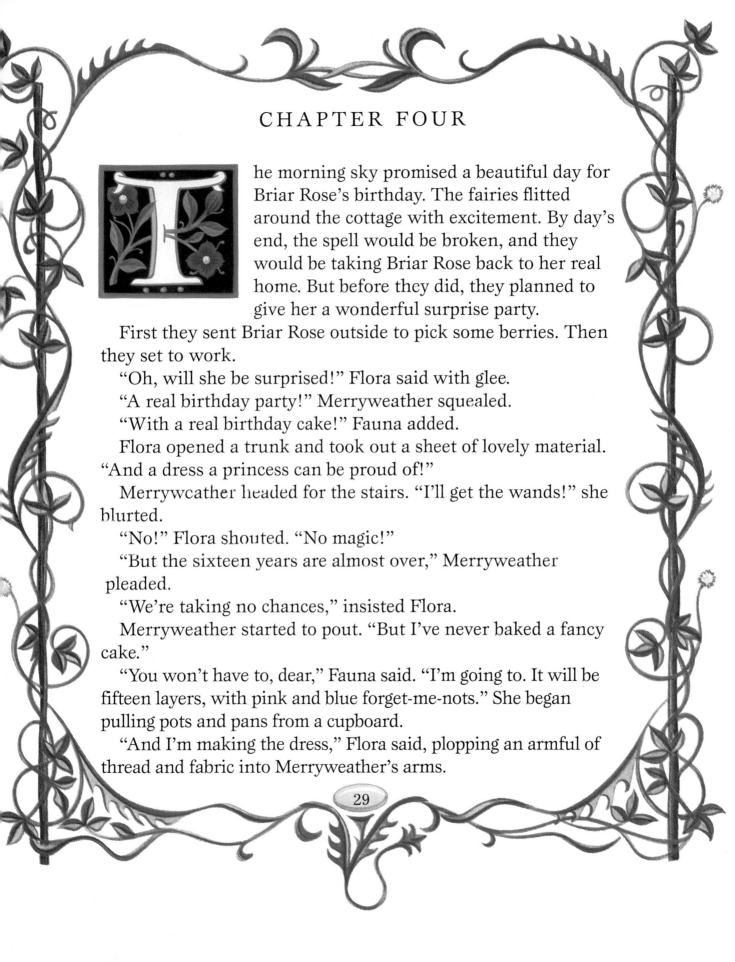

CHAPTER FOUR

he morning sky promised a beautiful day for Briar Rose's birthday. The fairies flitted around the cottage with excitement. By day's end, the spell would be broken, and they would be taking Briar Rose back to her real home. But before they did, they planned to give her a wonderful surprise party.

First they sent Briar Rose outside to pick some berries. Then they set to work.

"Oh, will she be surprised!" Flora said with glee.

"A real birthday party!" Merryweather squealed.

"With a real birthday cake!" Fauna added.

Flora opened a trunk and took out a sheet of lovely material. "And a dress a princess can be proud of!"

Merryweather headed for the stairs. "I'll get the wands!" she blurted.

"No!" Flora shouted. "No magic!"

"But the sixteen years are almost over," Merryweather pleaded.

"We're taking no chances," insisted Flora.

Merryweather started to pout. "But I've never baked a fancy cake."

"You won't have to, dear," Fauna said. "I'm going to. It will be fifteen layers, with pink and blue forget-me-nots." She began pulling pots and pans from a cupboard.

"And I'm making the dress," Flora said, plopping an armful of thread and fabric into Merryweather's arms.

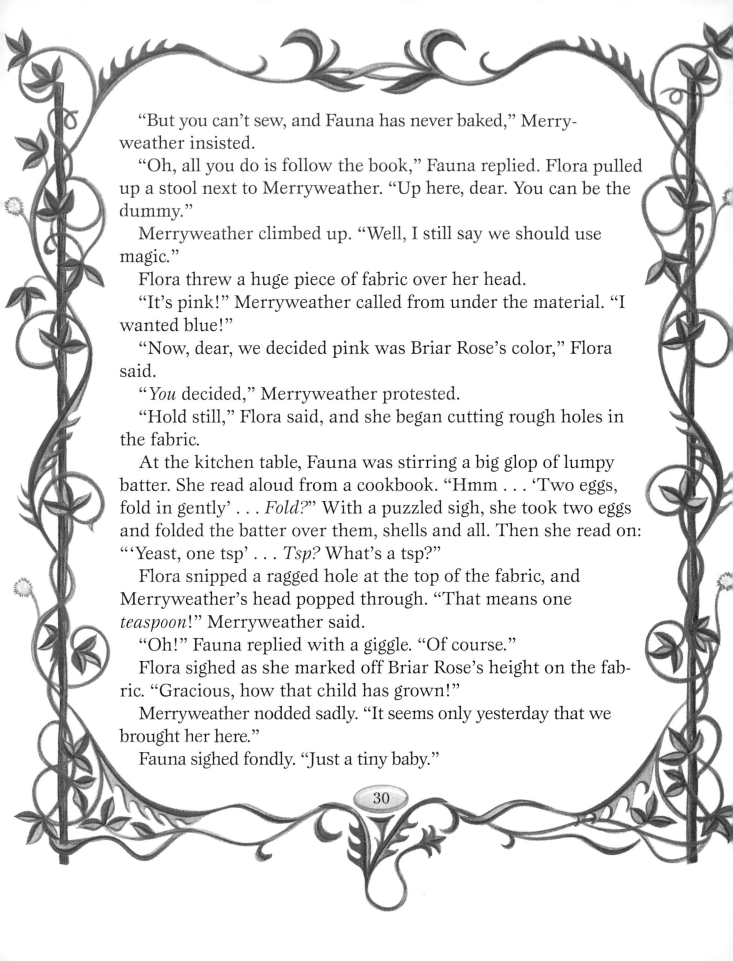

"But you can't sew, and Fauna has never baked," Merryweather insisted.

"Oh, all you do is follow the book," Fauna replied. Flora pulled up a stool next to Merryweather. "Up here, dear. You can be the dummy."

Merryweather climbed up. "Well, I still say we should use magic."

Flora threw a huge piece of fabric over her head.

"It's pink!" Merryweather called from under the material. "I wanted blue!"

"Now, dear, we decided pink was Briar Rose's color," Flora said.

"*You* decided," Merryweather protested.

"Hold still," Flora said, and she began cutting rough holes in the fabric.

At the kitchen table, Fauna was stirring a big glop of lumpy batter. She read aloud from a cookbook. "Hmm . . . 'Two eggs, fold in gently' . . . *Fold?*" With a puzzled sigh, she took two eggs and folded the batter over them, shells and all. Then she read on: "'Yeast, one tsp' . . . *Tsp?* What's a tsp?"

Flora snipped a ragged hole at the top of the fabric, and Merryweather's head popped through. "That means one *teaspoon*!" Merryweather said.

"Oh!" Fauna replied with a giggle. "Of course."

Flora sighed as she marked off Briar Rose's height on the fabric. "Gracious, how that child has grown!"

Merryweather nodded sadly. "It seems only yesterday that we brought her here."

Fauna sighed fondly. "Just a tiny baby."

"After today she'll be a princess," Merryweather sniffled, "and we won't have any Briar Rose."

Fauna's happy expression melted. "Oh, Flora!" she cried.

Flora fought back tears. "Now, now, now, we . . . we . . . we all knew this day had to come. . . ."

"But why did it have to come so soon?" Fauna asked tearfully.

Now all three of them were on the verge of weeping. Finally Flora cleared her throat and said, "Ah, good gracious, we're acting like ninnies! Come on, she'll be back before we get started!" Quietly the three fairies went back to work.

Not far away, Briar Rose stepped lightly through the woods, an empty wicker basket on her arm bouncing along with each step. The sunlight gently warmed her face, and the smell of spring blossoms was tart and sweet. Through the trees came the happy twittering and piping of birds. Spinning around, Briar Rose began to sing along in a high, clear voice.

In every burrow and every hollow log, the animals of the forest listened. So lovely was Briar Rose's voice that even the birds stopped to hear her. Before long she had her own private audience: a squirrel, a bluebird, a cardinal, two rabbits, even an old owl.

Clear across the forest, someone else was enchanted by her voice, too—someone kind and handsome—a young man dressed in the finest silk clothing. As he dashed along on his great white horse, Briar Rose's song reached his ears.

"Whoa, Samson!" he called to his horse. "Do you hear that? How beautiful! What is it? Let's find out."

But Samson had a mind of his own. He wouldn't budge.

"Aw, come on," the young man said with a smile. "For an extra bucket of oats and a few carrots?"

Samson took off like a shot. The young man whooped with joy as Samson leapt high over one log, then another, then . . .

BONK!

Samson stopped short. Above him was a large tree branch— and there was no one in the saddle anymore. He turned around to look for his master.

The young man was sitting in a pond, looking like an over-grown frog. Samson hung his head in embarrassment.

With a shake of his soggy head, the young man said simply, "No carrots!"

Dozens of forest animals now surrounded Briar Rose as she continued to pick berries and sing. Pairs of birds were singing sweetly to each other. But as Briar Rose watched them, she grew sad. She wished *she* had someone special to sing to.

She sat down by a pond and dipped her feet in. Through the trees, a castle loomed in the distance. Maybe a young prince lived there, she thought, or even a stablehand—*someone* she could share her happiness with.

"Oh, dear," she said with a sigh, "why do they still treat me like a child?"

"*Who?*" the owl hooted.

"Aunt Flora and Fauna and Merryweather," Briar Rose replied. "They never want me to meet anyone." She looked around at the sympathetic eyes around her and smiled. "But you know something? I fooled them. I have met someone!"

"*Who? Who?*" the owl repeated.

"Oh . . . a prince," she said.

The birds lighted on branches and stared. The chipmunks and squirrels quickly gathered at her feet.

"He's tall and handsome," Briar Rose said. "And *so* romantic. We walk together and talk together, and just before we say good-bye, he takes me in his arms and—"

The animals leaned forward, their eyes wide with expectation. The only sound was the breeze rustling the trees.

Briar Rose sighed again. "And then I wake up," she said quietly, her shoulders slumping.

The animals sat back, as disappointed as Briar Rose.

"Yes, it's only a dream," she said. "But they say if you dream a thing more than once, it's sure to come true—and I've seen him so many times!"

Briar Rose was so lost in her thoughts that she didn't notice a squirrel scurry along a tree branch and then return a few minutes later.

One by one the little squirrel got the attention of the cardinal, the bluebird, the two rabbits, and the owl. Quietly they slipped away to another part of the woods.

There they found another small pond and a young man drying his clothes on a branch.

"You know, Samson," the young man said, "that voice was too beautiful to be real. Maybe it was a mysterious being. . . ."

He had his back to the animals. His cap and cape were on the branch, his two boots on the ground. Quickly the squirrel ducked under the cap and carried it away. The birds and the owl flew off with the cape, and each rabbit hopped away with one boot.

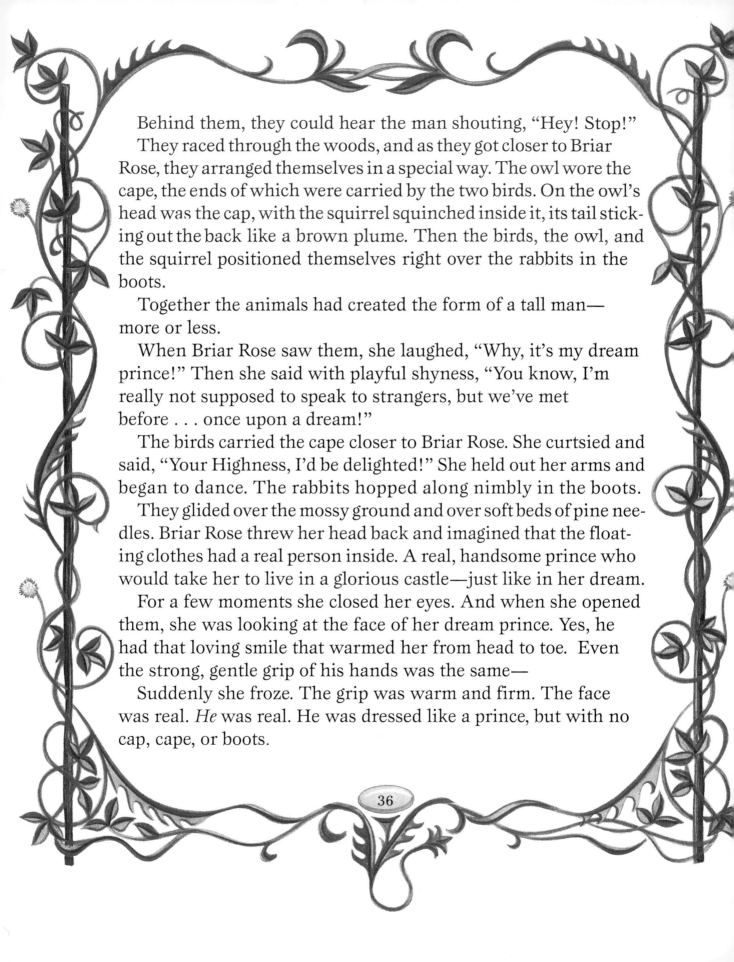

Behind them, they could hear the man shouting, "Hey! Stop!"

They raced through the woods, and as they got closer to Briar Rose, they arranged themselves in a special way. The owl wore the cape, the ends of which were carried by the two birds. On the owl's head was the cap, with the squirrel squinched inside it, its tail sticking out the back like a brown plume. Then the birds, the owl, and the squirrel positioned themselves right over the rabbits in the boots.

Together the animals had created the form of a tall man—more or less.

When Briar Rose saw them, she laughed, "Why, it's my dream prince!" Then she said with playful shyness, "You know, I'm really not supposed to speak to strangers, but we've met before . . . once upon a dream!"

The birds carried the cape closer to Briar Rose. She curtsied and said, "Your Highness, I'd be delighted!" She held out her arms and began to dance. The rabbits hopped along nimbly in the boots.

They glided over the mossy ground and over soft beds of pine needles. Briar Rose threw her head back and imagined that the floating clothes had a real person inside. A real, handsome prince who would take her to live in a glorious castle—just like in her dream.

For a few moments she closed her eyes. And when she opened them, she was looking at the face of her dream prince. Yes, he had that loving smile that warmed her from head to toe. Even the strong, gentle grip of his hands was the same—

Suddenly she froze. The grip was warm and firm. The face was real. *He* was real. He was dressed like a prince, but with no cap, cape, or boots.

And he was the very first person Briar Rose had ever seen
besides her aunts.

"Oh!" she cried out, backing away.

"I'm awfully sorry," the young man said. "I didn't mean to
frighten you."

"It wasn't that," she replied. "It's just that you're a . . . a . . .
stranger."

The young man smiled. "But don't you remember? We've met
before."

"We . . . we have?"

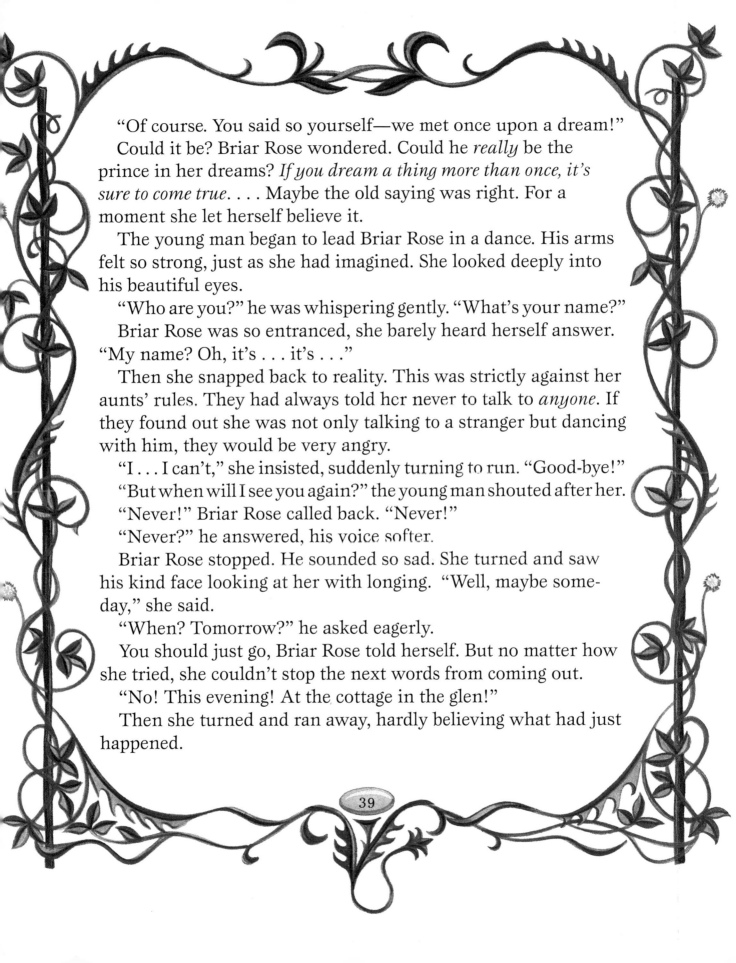

"Of course. You said so yourself—we met once upon a dream!"

Could it be? Briar Rose wondered. Could he *really* be the prince in her dreams? *If you dream a thing more than once, it's sure to come true. . . .* Maybe the old saying was right. For a moment she let herself believe it.

The young man began to lead Briar Rose in a dance. His arms felt so strong, just as she had imagined. She looked deeply into his beautiful eyes.

"Who are you?" he was whispering gently. "What's your name?"

Briar Rose was so entranced, she barely heard herself answer. "My name? Oh, it's . . . it's . . ."

Then she snapped back to reality. This was strictly against her aunts' rules. They had always told her never to talk to *anyone*. If they found out she was not only talking to a stranger but dancing with him, they would be very angry.

"I . . . I can't," she insisted, suddenly turning to run. "Good-bye!"

"But when will I see you again?" the young man shouted after her.

"Never!" Briar Rose called back. "Never!"

"Never?" he answered, his voice softer.

Briar Rose stopped. He sounded so sad. She turned and saw his kind face looking at her with longing. "Well, maybe some-day," she said.

"When? Tomorrow?" he asked eagerly.

You should just go, Briar Rose told herself. But no matter how she tried, she couldn't stop the next words from coming out.

"No! This evening! At the cottage in the glen!"

Then she turned and ran away, hardly believing what had just happened.

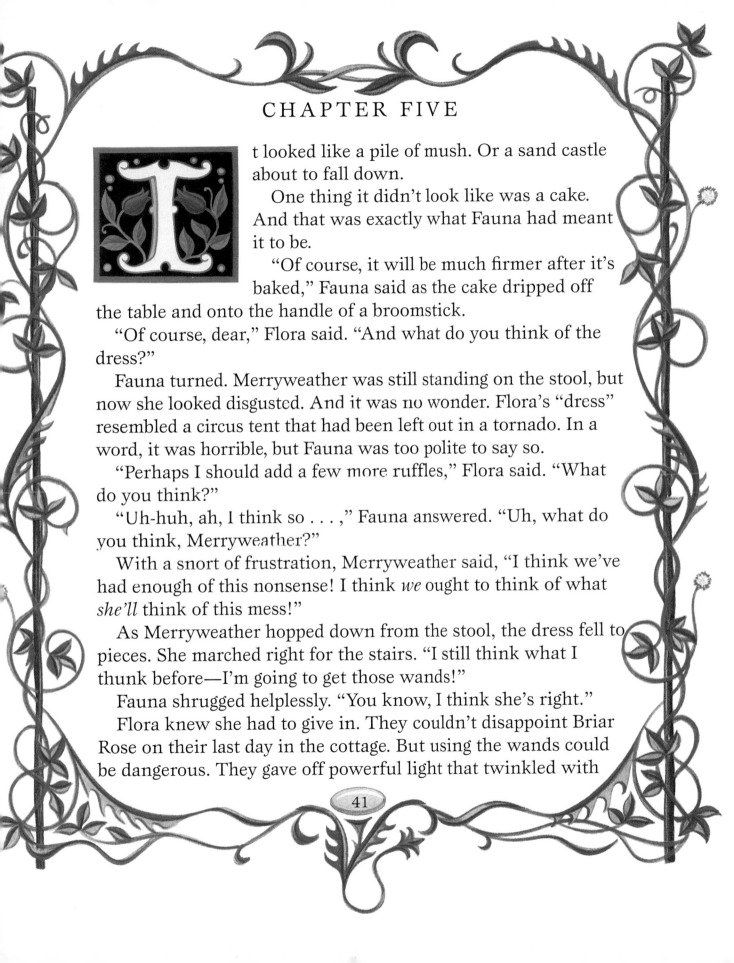

CHAPTER FIVE

It looked like a pile of mush. Or a sand castle about to fall down.

One thing it didn't look like was a cake. And that was exactly what Fauna had meant it to be.

"Of course, it will be much firmer after it's baked," Fauna said as the cake dripped off the table and onto the handle of a broomstick.

"Of course, dear," Flora said. "And what do you think of the dress?"

Fauna turned. Merryweather was still standing on the stool, but now she looked disgusted. And it was no wonder. Flora's "dress" resembled a circus tent that had been left out in a tornado. In a word, it was horrible, but Fauna was too polite to say so.

"Perhaps I should add a few more ruffles," Flora said. "What do you think?"

"Uh-huh, ah, I think so . . . ," Fauna answered. "Uh, what do you think, Merryweather?"

With a snort of frustration, Merryweather said, "I think we've had enough of this nonsense! I think *we* ought to think of what *she'll* think of this mess!"

As Merryweather hopped down from the stool, the dress fell to pieces. She marched right for the stairs. "I still think what I thunk before—I'm going to get those wands!"

Fauna shrugged helplessly. "You know, I think she's right."

Flora knew she had to give in. They couldn't disappoint Briar Rose on their last day in the cottage. But using the wands could be dangerous. They gave off powerful light that twinkled with

magic dust. If any of that light were to escape the cottage, maybe, just maybe, someone outside would spot it. Surely Maleficent's spies were still searching for the princess.

"All right," Flora said. "But we can't take any chances. Lock the doors! Close the windows! Plug up every cranny!"

Merryweather ran back downstairs with the wands. In a flurry the fairies raced around, following Flora's instructions. They made sure even the tiniest knothole in the cottage wall was plugged with a rag.

Then they each took hold of the tiny magic sticks that were once so familiar to them. With a grand wave, they really began to prepare for the party.

Zzzing! Merryweather made the bucket, mop, and broom burst to life. They bustled about, cleaning the cottage.

Zzzing! Fauna created a magnificent cake out of the ingredients on the table.

Zzzing! Flora made the material come together to form a stunning pink gown.

Merryweather took one look at the gown and cried out, "Oh no, not pink! Make it blue!" With a wave of her wand, the gown's color instantly changed to blue.

"Merryweather!" Flora scolded. "Make it pink!" *Zzzing!* She waved her wand and changed it back to pink.

Zzzing! Merryweather made it blue again.

Zzzing! Flora made it pink.

Zzzing! Blue!

Zzzing! Pink!

Blue and pink magic dust shot through the cottage, bouncing

off walls and mirrors. Even Flora's and Merryweather's own dresses changed colors. Before long they were shrieking with laughter. After sixteen years, it felt so good to use their wands again.

Had Flora and Merryweather been a little less exhilarated and a little more careful, they would have seen the magic dust shooting into the one place they had not thought to seal up—the chimney. They would have seen the dust fly straight up the flue and into the sky like pink and blue fireworks.

Someone did notice, though—Maleficent's pet raven, circling high above the forest. With great interest, he flew toward the cottage to investigate.

As he landed silently on the chimney, the fireworks disappeared. Inside the cottage, the fairies stopped what they were doing. "Shhh!" Fauna said. "Listen!"

They could hear the sound of Briar Rose's sweet singing in the distance. With her view of the sky blocked by the forest's thick trees, she had not seen the magic dust.

"Rose is back!" Flora exclaimed. "Enough of this foolishness."

The fairies sprang into action. Fauna lit the candles on the cake. Flora turned Briar Rose's dress pink, then grabbed Fauna by the hand. The two of them ran to hide on the stairs.

Merryweather waved her wand to make the dishes clean themselves and jump into the cupboard. As she scurried toward the stairs, she turned the dress blue.

"Aunt Flora!" came Briar Rose's voice from outside.

Flora's eyes widened. "Good gracious! Who left the mop running?"

Sure enough, the mop was still in the middle of the floor, doing a dance as it cleaned up.

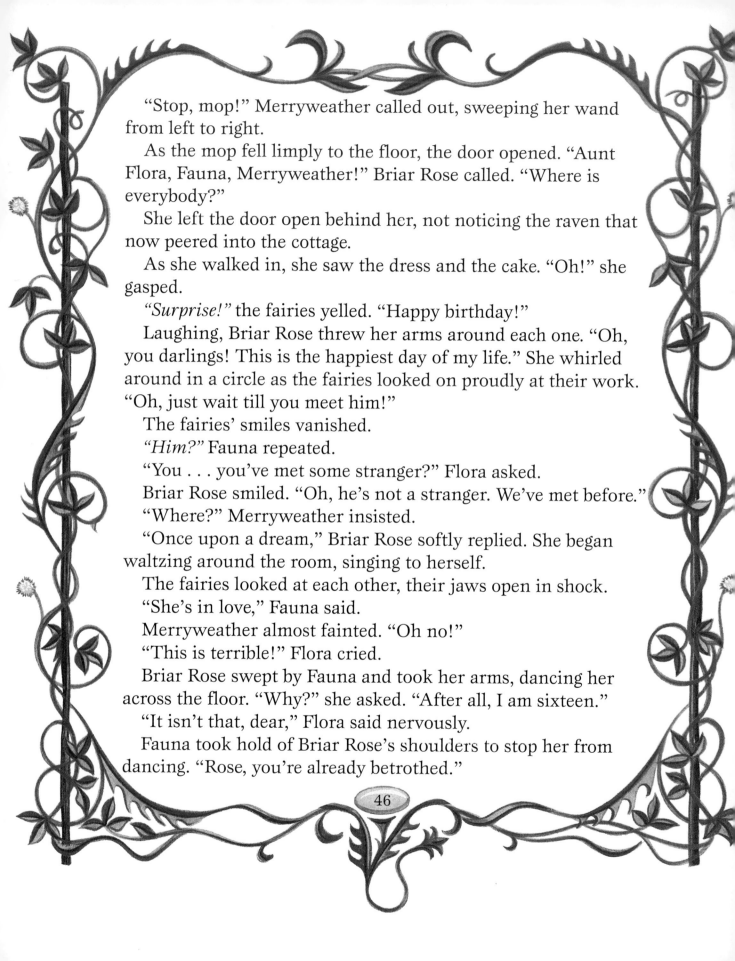

"Stop, mop!" Merryweather called out, sweeping her wand from left to right.

As the mop fell limply to the floor, the door opened. "Aunt Flora, Fauna, Merryweather!" Briar Rose called. "Where is everybody?"

She left the door open behind her, not noticing the raven that now peered into the cottage.

As she walked in, she saw the dress and the cake. "Oh!" she gasped.

"*Surprise!*" the fairies yelled. "Happy birthday!"

Laughing, Briar Rose threw her arms around each one. "Oh, you darlings! This is the happiest day of my life." She whirled around in a circle as the fairies looked on proudly at their work. "Oh, just wait till you meet him!"

The fairies' smiles vanished.

"*Him?*" Fauna repeated.

"You . . . you've met some stranger?" Flora asked.

Briar Rose smiled. "Oh, he's not a stranger. We've met before."

"Where?" Merryweather insisted.

"Once upon a dream," Briar Rose softly replied. She began waltzing around the room, singing to herself.

The fairies looked at each other, their jaws open in shock.

"She's in love," Fauna said.

Merryweather almost fainted. "Oh no!"

"This is terrible!" Flora cried.

Briar Rose swept by Fauna and took her arms, dancing her across the floor. "Why?" she asked. "After all, I am sixteen."

"It isn't that, dear," Flora said nervously.

Fauna took hold of Briar Rose's shoulders to stop her from dancing. "Rose, you're already betrothed."

46

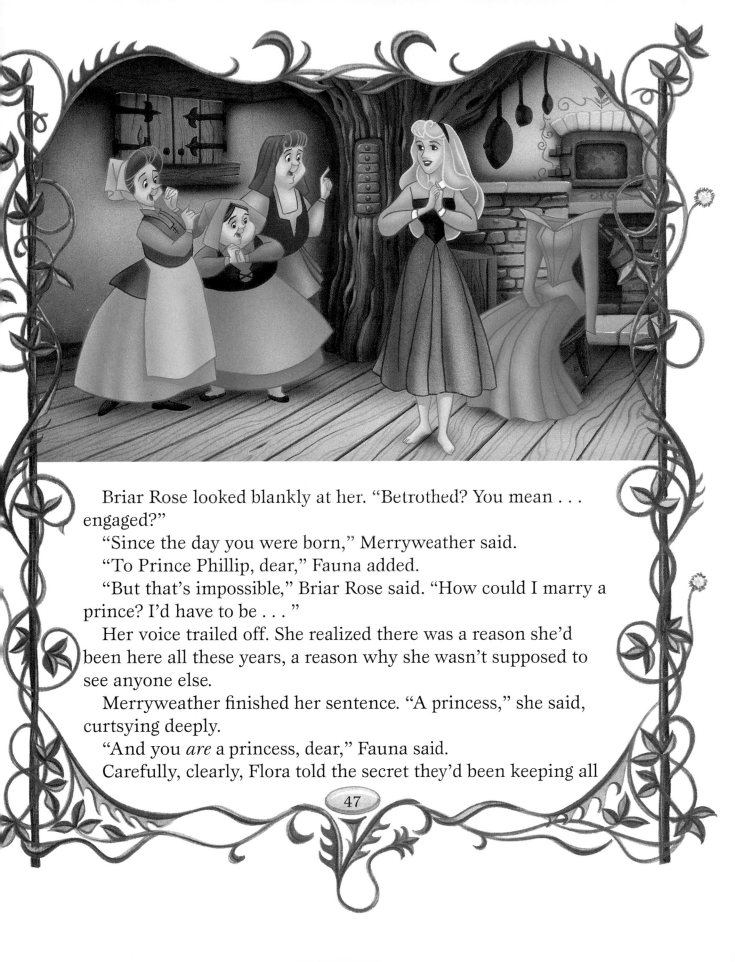

Briar Rose looked blankly at her. "Betrothed? You mean . . . engaged?"

"Since the day you were born," Merryweather said.

"To Prince Phillip, dear," Fauna added.

"But that's impossible," Briar Rose said. "How could I marry a prince? I'd have to be . . ."

Her voice trailed off. She realized there was a reason she'd been here all these years, a reason why she wasn't supposed to see anyone else.

Merryweather finished her sentence. "A princess," she said, curtsying deeply.

"And you *are* a princess, dear," Fauna said.

Carefully, clearly, Flora told the secret they'd been keeping all

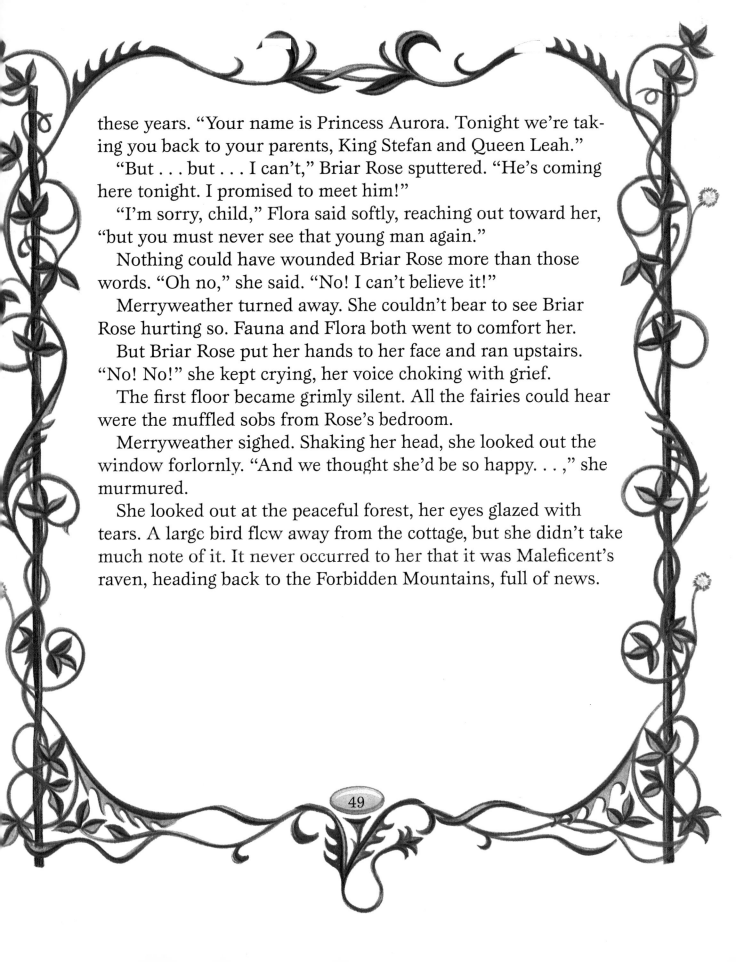

these years. "Your name is Princess Aurora. Tonight we're taking you back to your parents, King Stefan and Queen Leah."

"But . . . but . . . I can't," Briar Rose sputtered. "He's coming here tonight. I promised to meet him!"

"I'm sorry, child," Flora said softly, reaching out toward her, "but you must never see that young man again."

Nothing could have wounded Briar Rose more than those words. "Oh no," she said. "No! I can't believe it!"

Merryweather turned away. She couldn't bear to see Briar Rose hurting so. Fauna and Flora both went to comfort her.

But Briar Rose put her hands to her face and ran upstairs. "No! No!" she kept crying, her voice choking with grief.

The first floor became grimly silent. All the fairies could hear were the muffled sobs from Rose's bedroom.

Merryweather sighed. Shaking her head, she looked out the window forlornly. "And we thought she'd be so happy. . . ," she murmured.

She looked out at the peaceful forest, her eyes glazed with tears. A large bird flew away from the cottage, but she didn't take much note of it. It never occurred to her that it was Maleficent's raven, heading back to the Forbidden Mountains, full of news.

CHAPTER SIX

ing Hubert gobbled down another piece of cake. Laid out before him was a feast fit for a king—two kings, to be exact. The royal table was overflowing, in celebration of Princess Aurora's return. But for all King Hubert's appetite, King Stefan had not eaten a thing.

He paced the floor anxiously, looking out the window for the hundredth time.

Outside, it was gloomier than ever. Maleficent's thunder practically shook the ground, which was a good sign. It was getting late, and soon Aurora's birthday would be over.

"No sign of her yet, Hubert," King Stefan said.

" 'Course not," King Hubert said in midchew. "There's a good half hour till sunset. Come, man, buck up! The battle's over. The girl's as good as here!"

King Stefan exhaled deeply. "I'm sorry, Hubert, but after sixteen years of worrying, never knowing . . ."

"All in the past!" King Hubert reassured him. Grabbing a bottle of wine, he poured two glasses. "Tonight we toast the future!"

They raised their glasses and clinked them together. "To the future, Hubert," King Stefan said, a smile growing across his face. "To the marriage of our children and the uniting of our kingdoms!"

"And to the new home, eh?" King Hubert said.

"New home?" King Stefan asked.

King Hubert snapped his fingers, and an attendant quickly ran over with a thick roll of parchment. As King Hubert unfurled

it, King Stefan stared in amazement. It was the plans for an enormous castle.

"Forty bedrooms, dining hall, honeymoon cottage—all built and ready to go!" King Hubert beamed proudly at the plans. "The lovebirds can move in tomorrow."

"Tomorrow?" King Stefan put his glass down in shock. "But Hubert, they're not even married."

"Ha! We'll take care of that tonight!" King Hubert poured some more wine and raised his glass again. "To the wedding!"

"Hold on, Hubert," King Stefan said. "I haven't even seen my daughter yet, and you're taking her away from me."

"You're getting my Phillip, aren't you?" King Hubert asked. "And we want to see our grandchildren, don't we?"

"Well, yes, of course," King Stefan replied. "But be reasonable. Aurora knows nothing about this, and it may come as something of a shock to her."

King Hubert suddenly smacked his glass down on the table. "Shock? My Phillip a shock? What's wrong with my Phillip?"

"Nothing," King Stefan protested. "I only meant—"

"Why, doesn't your daughter like my son?" King Hubert harrumphed. "I'm not so sure my son likes your daughter! I'm not sure my grandchildren want you for a grandfather!"

King Stefan was furious. "Now see here, you unreasonable, pompous, blustering old windbag!"

"*Windbag?*" King Hubert shouted. His face was red with anger. He reached out to grab a weapon—anything. The first thing his fingers clenched was a cooked fish. "On guard, sir!"

He thrust toward King Stefan with the fish. Grabbing a platter like a shield, King Stefan said, "I warn you, Hubert. This means war!"

52

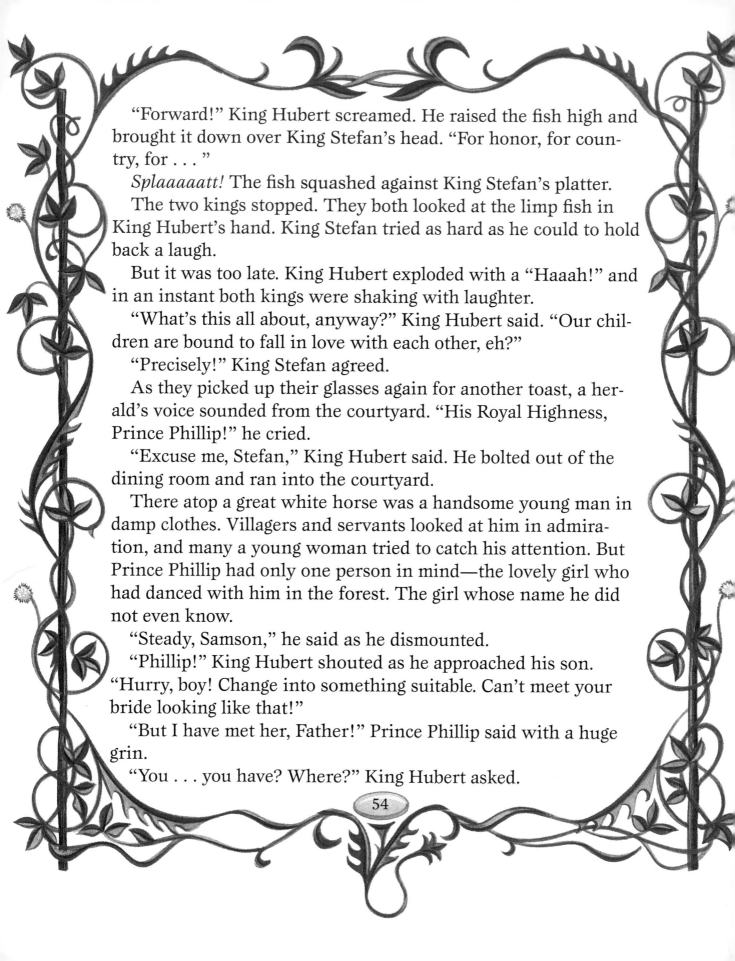

"Forward!" King Hubert screamed. He raised the fish high and brought it down over King Stefan's head. "For honor, for country, for . . ."

Splaaaaatt! The fish squashed against King Stefan's platter.

The two kings stopped. They both looked at the limp fish in King Hubert's hand. King Stefan tried as hard as he could to hold back a laugh.

But it was too late. King Hubert exploded with a "Haaah!" and in an instant both kings were shaking with laughter.

"What's this all about, anyway?" King Hubert said. "Our children are bound to fall in love with each other, eh?"

"Precisely!" King Stefan agreed.

As they picked up their glasses again for another toast, a herald's voice sounded from the courtyard. "His Royal Highness, Prince Phillip!" he cried.

"Excuse me, Stefan," King Hubert said. He bolted out of the dining room and ran into the courtyard.

There atop a great white horse was a handsome young man in damp clothes. Villagers and servants looked at him in admiration, and many a young woman tried to catch his attention. But Prince Phillip had only one person in mind—the lovely girl who had danced with him in the forest. The girl whose name he did not even know.

"Steady, Samson," he said as he dismounted.

"Phillip!" King Hubert shouted as he approached his son. "Hurry, boy! Change into something suitable. Can't meet your bride looking like that!"

"But I have met her, Father!" Prince Phillip said with a huge grin.

"You . . . you have? Where?" King Hubert asked.

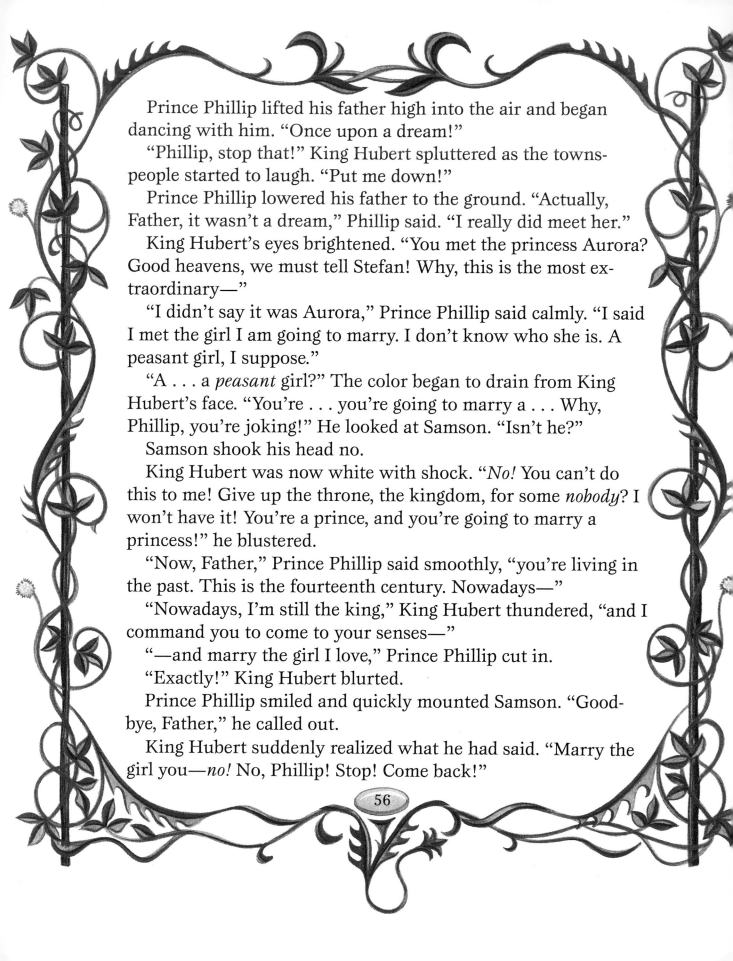

Prince Phillip lifted his father high into the air and began dancing with him. "Once upon a dream!"

"Phillip, stop that!" King Hubert spluttered as the townspeople started to laugh. "Put me down!"

Prince Phillip lowered his father to the ground. "Actually, Father, it wasn't a dream," Phillip said. "I really did meet her."

King Hubert's eyes brightened. "You met the princess Aurora? Good heavens, we must tell Stefan! Why, this is the most extraordinary—"

"I didn't say it was Aurora," Prince Phillip said calmly. "I said I met the girl I am going to marry. I don't know who she is. A peasant girl, I suppose."

"A . . . a *peasant* girl?" The color began to drain from King Hubert's face. "You're . . . you're going to marry a . . . Why, Phillip, you're joking!" He looked at Samson. "Isn't he?"

Samson shook his head no.

King Hubert was now white with shock. "*No!* You can't do this to me! Give up the throne, the kingdom, for some *nobody*? I won't have it! You're a prince, and you're going to marry a princess!" he blustered.

"Now, Father," Prince Phillip said smoothly, "you're living in the past. This is the fourteenth century. Nowadays—"

"Nowadays, I'm still the king," King Hubert thundered, "and I command you to come to your senses—"

"—and marry the girl I love," Prince Phillip cut in.

"Exactly!" King Hubert blurted.

Prince Phillip smiled and quickly mounted Samson. "Goodbye, Father," he called out.

King Hubert suddenly realized what he had said. "Marry the girl you—*no!* No, Phillip! Stop! Come back!"

But Prince Phillip was already on his way. He wasn't going to have his marriage arranged for him. Sixteen years ago, Princess Aurora had been a little baby. He had no idea what she was like now, but he knew she couldn't be lovelier and sweeter than the girl he'd met today.

This evening, at the cottage in the glen was what the girl had said. And Phillip intended to be there.

CHAPTER SEVEN

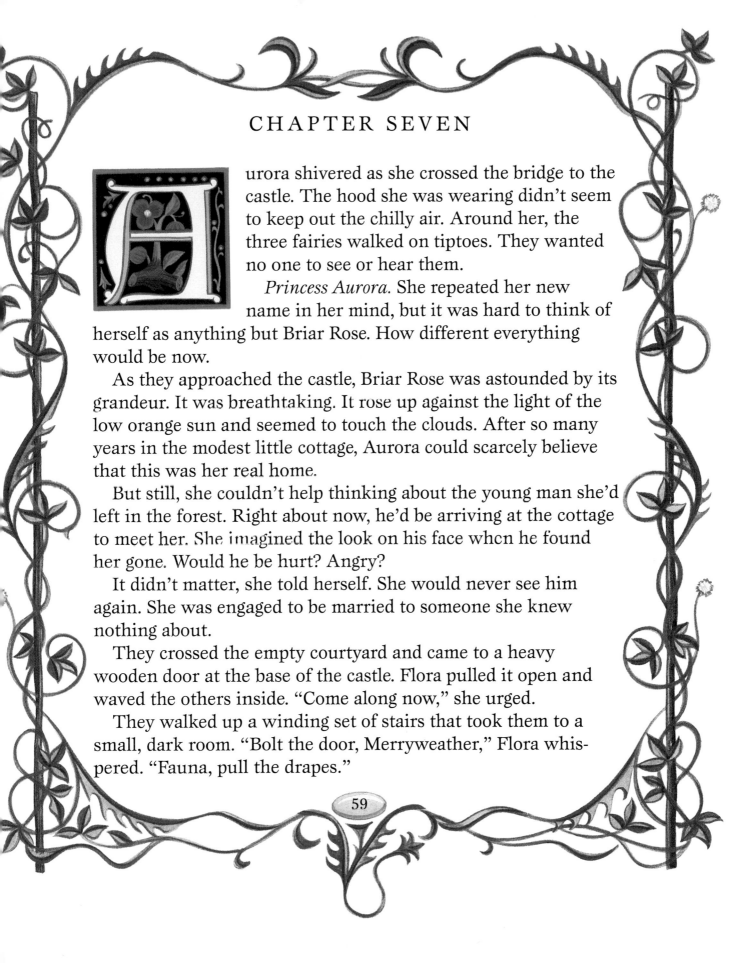

urora shivered as she crossed the bridge to the castle. The hood she was wearing didn't seem to keep out the chilly air. Around her, the three fairies walked on tiptoes. They wanted no one to see or hear them.

Princess Aurora. She repeated her new name in her mind, but it was hard to think of herself as anything but Briar Rose. How different everything would be now.

As they approached the castle, Briar Rose was astounded by its grandeur. It was breathtaking. It rose up against the light of the low orange sun and seemed to touch the clouds. After so many years in the modest little cottage, Aurora could scarcely believe that this was her real home.

But still, she couldn't help thinking about the young man she'd left in the forest. Right about now, he'd be arriving at the cottage to meet her. She imagined the look on his face when he found her gone. Would he be hurt? Angry?

It didn't matter, she told herself. She would never see him again. She was engaged to be married to someone she knew nothing about.

They crossed the empty courtyard and came to a heavy wooden door at the base of the castle. Flora pulled it open and waved the others inside. "Come along now," she urged.

They walked up a winding set of stairs that took them to a small, dark room. "Bolt the door, Merryweather," Flora whispered. "Fauna, pull the drapes."

As the two fairies scurried about, Flora gently led Aurora to a seat before a large mirror. Waving her magic wand, she chanted,

This one last gift, dear child, for thee,
The symbol of thy royalty:
A crown to wear in grace and beauty,
As is thy right and royal duty!

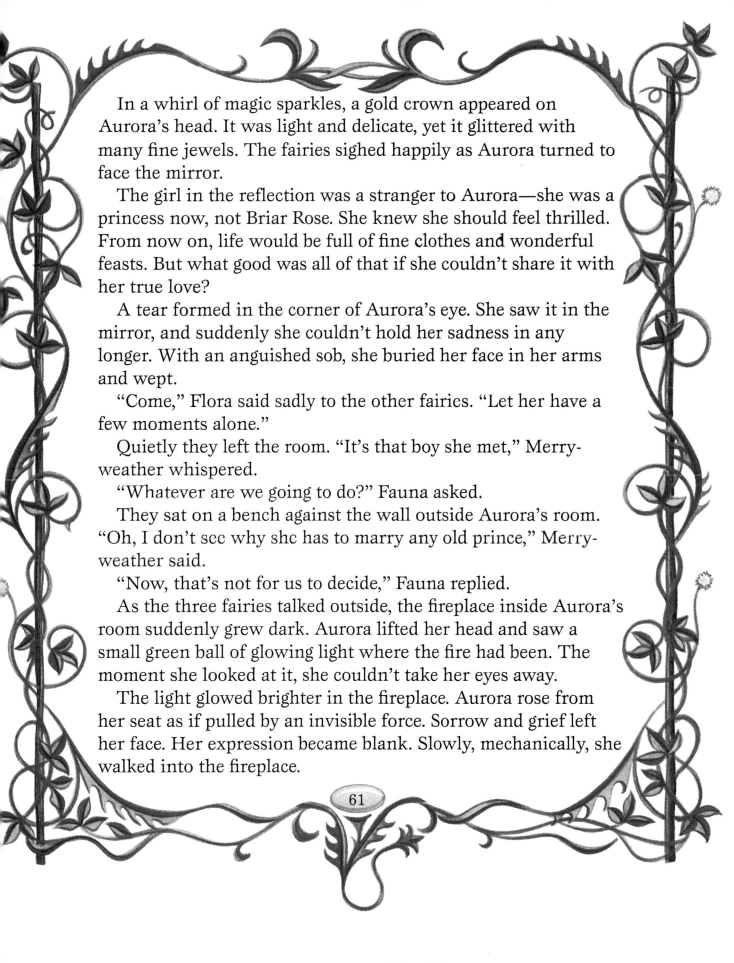

In a whirl of magic sparkles, a gold crown appeared on Aurora's head. It was light and delicate, yet it glittered with many fine jewels. The fairies sighed happily as Aurora turned to face the mirror.

The girl in the reflection was a stranger to Aurora—she was a princess now, not Briar Rose. She knew she should feel thrilled. From now on, life would be full of fine clothes and wonderful feasts. But what good was all of that if she couldn't share it with her true love?

A tear formed in the corner of Aurora's eye. She saw it in the mirror, and suddenly she couldn't hold her sadness in any longer. With an anguished sob, she buried her face in her arms and wept.

"Come," Flora said sadly to the other fairies. "Let her have a few moments alone."

Quietly they left the room. "It's that boy she met," Merry-weather whispered.

"Whatever are we going to do?" Fauna asked.

They sat on a bench against the wall outside Aurora's room. "Oh, I don't see why she has to marry any old prince," Merry-weather said.

"Now, that's not for us to decide," Fauna replied.

As the three fairies talked outside, the fireplace inside Aurora's room suddenly grew dark. Aurora lifted her head and saw a small green ball of glowing light where the fire had been. The moment she looked at it, she couldn't take her eyes away.

The light glowed brighter in the fireplace. Aurora rose from her seat as if pulled by an invisible force. Sorrow and grief left her face. Her expression became blank. Slowly, mechanically, she walked into the fireplace.

Shrouded in black, a dark image appeared around the light. It leered with evil triumph, then disappeared. Aurora's glazed eyes did not notice the unmistakable grin of Maleficent.

Outside, the thunder and lightning surrounding Maleficent's castle stopped for the first time in sixteen years.

It was Flora who first noticed the change in the weather. In the strange quiet, her ears picked up the sound of shuffling feet inside Aurora's room—and a low, familiar laugh she hadn't heard in years. "Listen!" she cried in alarm. "Maleficent!"

Merryweather and Fauna jumped up and ran for the door, shouting, "Rose! Rose!"

They all burst into the room just in time to see Aurora step through an archway at the back wall of the fireplace. As she stepped into the corridor beyond, the solid wall reappeared. Aurora was gone.

The fairies pounded the wall with their fists. "Oh, why did we leave her alone?" Fauna moaned.

"Oh . . . here!" Flora said, remembering her wand. She waved it once, and the wall disappeared.

The fairies raced through. They found a stone staircase that spiraled up toward the castle's tallest tower. A smoky green light flickered in the stairwell's shadows, then disappeared.

"Rose!" they yelled, running up to the next floor. "Where are you?" Surely Maleficent was taking the princess into one of the castle's many empty rooms—but which one? On each floor there were so many doors and so many other staircases going in so many different directions. They scattered around, trying each one.

In the middle of a small, empty room at the top of the tower, the green light stopped moving. So did Aurora. The frantic foot-

falls of the fairies echoed faintly outside the room, but Aurora was not aware of them. She stared blankly as the light transformed. It began to grow and change shape until at last a spinning wheel stood before her. On it, a long spindle glistened with unearthly light.

Slowly she reached her finger toward it.

"Rose!" came the fairies' voices. *"Don't touch anything!"*

The words were loud and strong. They broke through the

witch's spell ever so slightly. Aurora drew back her hand.

"*Touch the spindle!*" Maleficent hissed, invisible in the darkened room. "*Touch it, I say!*"

Aurora's eyes glazed over. Once again, she reached toward the blinding white pinpoint.

Out in the hallway, Merryweather heard the witch's horrible voice. "In here!" Merryweather cried, pointing to the room.

Together the fairies barged in.

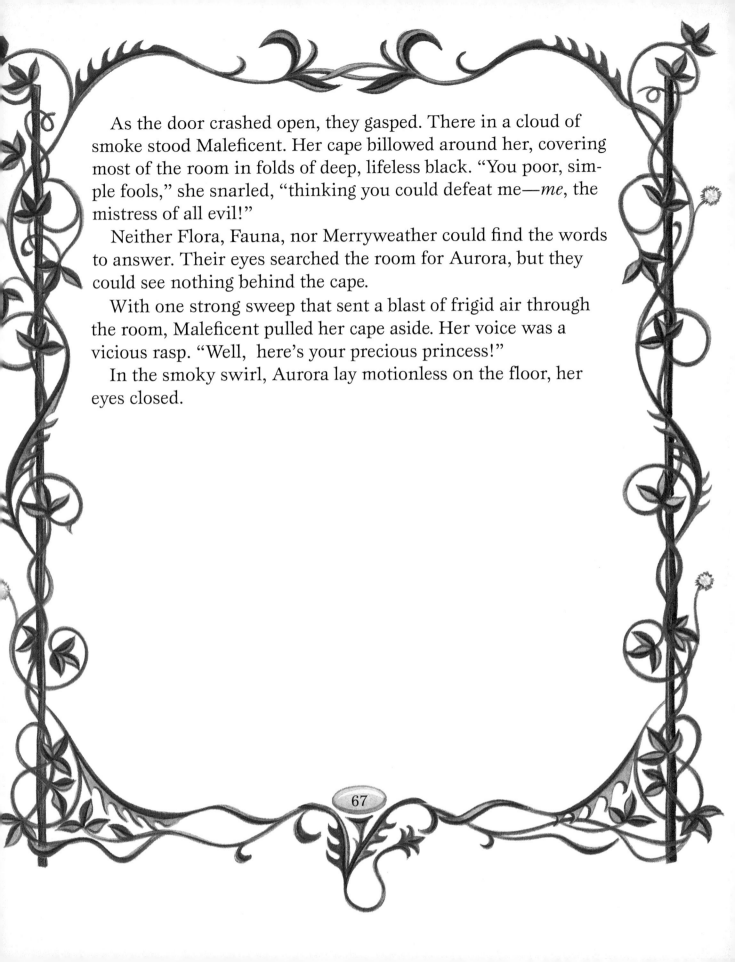

As the door crashed open, they gasped. There in a cloud of smoke stood Maleficent. Her cape billowed around her, covering most of the room in folds of deep, lifeless black. "You poor, simple fools," she snarled, "thinking you could defeat me—*me*, the mistress of all evil!"

Neither Flora, Fauna, nor Merryweather could find the words to answer. Their eyes searched the room for Aurora, but they could see nothing behind the cape.

With one strong sweep that sent a blast of frigid air through the room, Maleficent pulled her cape aside. Her voice was a vicious rasp. "Well, here's your precious princess!"

In the smoky swirl, Aurora lay motionless on the floor, her eyes closed.

CHAPTER EIGHT

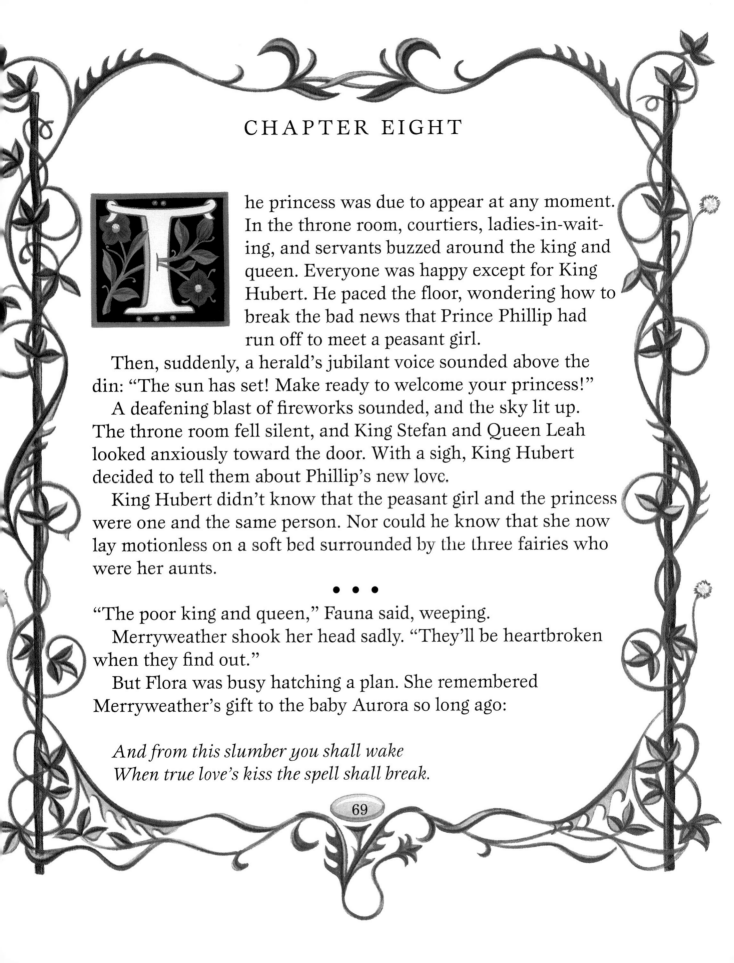

The princess was due to appear at any moment. In the throne room, courtiers, ladies-in-waiting, and servants buzzed around the king and queen. Everyone was happy except for King Hubert. He paced the floor, wondering how to break the bad news that Prince Phillip had run off to meet a peasant girl.

Then, suddenly, a herald's jubilant voice sounded above the din: "The sun has set! Make ready to welcome your princess!"

A deafening blast of fireworks sounded, and the sky lit up. The throne room fell silent, and King Stefan and Queen Leah looked anxiously toward the door. With a sigh, King Hubert decided to tell them about Phillip's new love.

King Hubert didn't know that the peasant girl and the princess were one and the same person. Nor could he know that she now lay motionless on a soft bed surrounded by the three fairies who were her aunts.

• • •

"The poor king and queen," Fauna said, weeping.

Merryweather shook her head sadly. "They'll be heartbroken when they find out."

But Flora was busy hatching a plan. She remembered Merryweather's gift to the baby Aurora so long ago:

And from this slumber you shall wake
When true love's kiss the spell shall break.

69

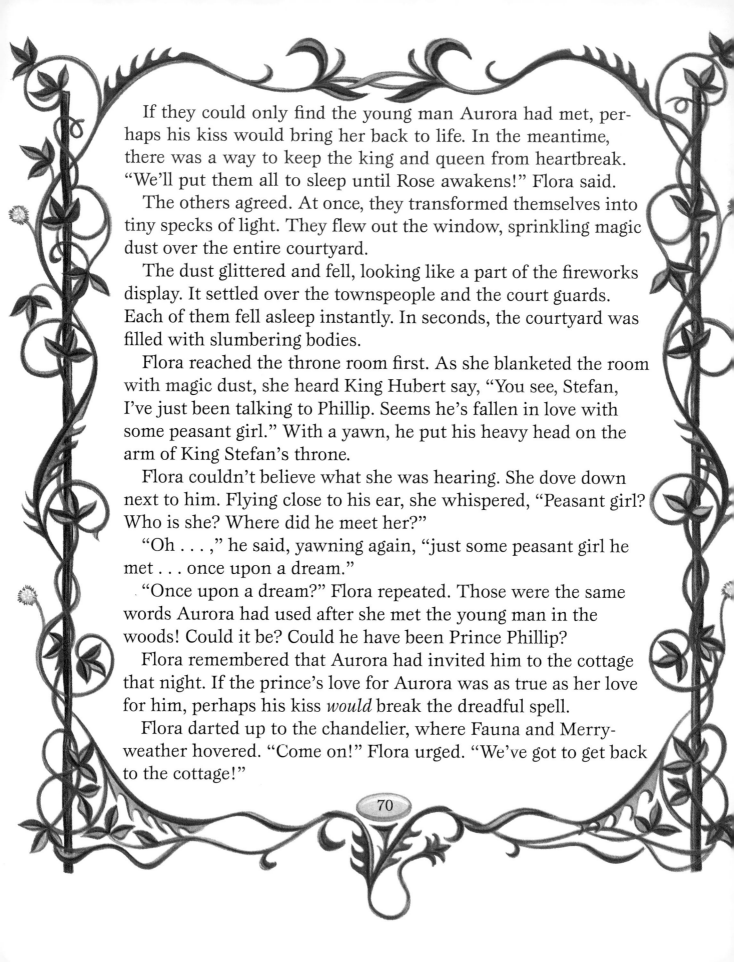

If they could only find the young man Aurora had met, perhaps his kiss would bring her back to life. In the meantime, there was a way to keep the king and queen from heartbreak. "We'll put them all to sleep until Rose awakens!" Flora said.

The others agreed. At once, they transformed themselves into tiny specks of light. They flew out the window, sprinkling magic dust over the entire courtyard.

The dust glittered and fell, looking like a part of the fireworks display. It settled over the townspeople and the court guards. Each of them fell asleep instantly. In seconds, the courtyard was filled with slumbering bodies.

Flora reached the throne room first. As she blanketed the room with magic dust, she heard King Hubert say, "You see, Stefan, I've just been talking to Phillip. Seems he's fallen in love with some peasant girl." With a yawn, he put his heavy head on the arm of King Stefan's throne.

Flora couldn't believe what she was hearing. She dove down next to him. Flying close to his ear, she whispered, "Peasant girl? Who is she? Where did he meet her?"

"Oh . . . ," he said, yawning again, "just some peasant girl he met . . . once upon a dream."

"Once upon a dream?" Flora repeated. Those were the same words Aurora had used after she met the young man in the woods! Could it be? Could he have been Prince Phillip?

Flora remembered that Aurora had invited him to the cottage that night. If the prince's love for Aurora was as true as her love for him, perhaps his kiss *would* break the dreadful spell.

Flora darted up to the chandelier, where Fauna and Merryweather hovered. "Come on!" Flora urged. "We've got to get back to the cottage!"

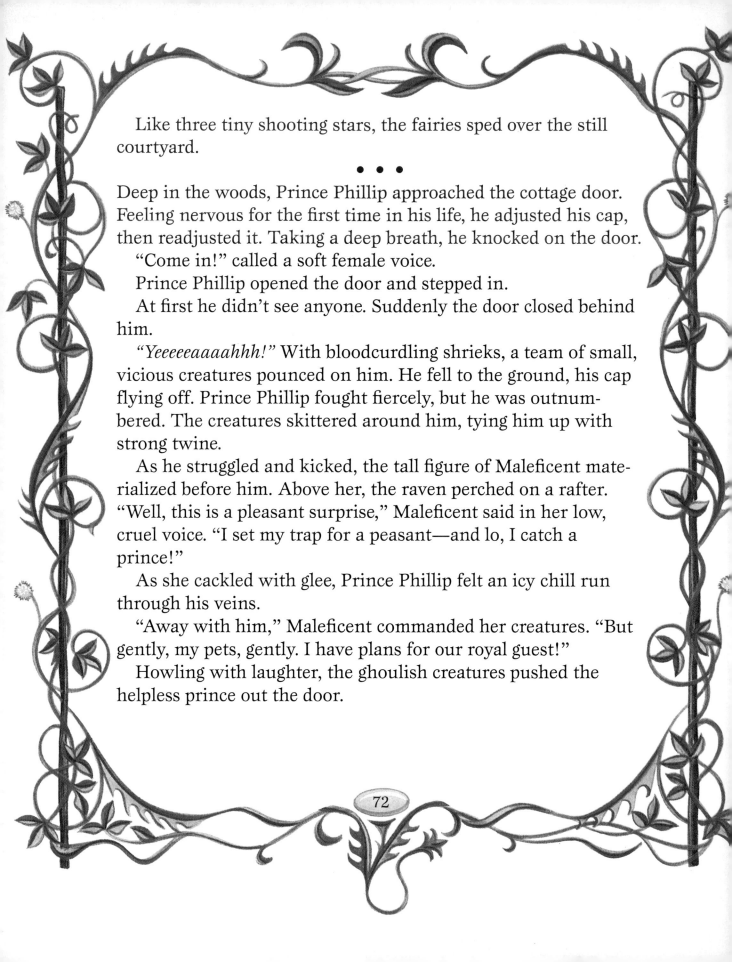

Like three tiny shooting stars, the fairies sped over the still courtyard.

• • •

Deep in the woods, Prince Phillip approached the cottage door. Feeling nervous for the first time in his life, he adjusted his cap, then readjusted it. Taking a deep breath, he knocked on the door.

"Come in!" called a soft female voice.

Prince Phillip opened the door and stepped in.

At first he didn't see anyone. Suddenly the door closed behind him.

"Yeeeeeaaaahhh!" With bloodcurdling shrieks, a team of small, vicious creatures pounced on him. He fell to the ground, his cap flying off. Prince Phillip fought fiercely, but he was outnumbered. The creatures skittered around him, tying him up with strong twine.

As he struggled and kicked, the tall figure of Maleficent materialized before him. Above her, the raven perched on a rafter. "Well, this is a pleasant surprise," Maleficent said in her low, cruel voice. "I set my trap for a peasant—and lo, I catch a prince!"

As she cackled with glee, Prince Phillip felt an icy chill run through his veins.

"Away with him," Maleficent commanded her creatures. "But gently, my pets, gently. I have plans for our royal guest!"

Howling with laughter, the ghoulish creatures pushed the helpless prince out the door.

CHAPTER NINE

By the time the fairies got to the cottage, all that was left of Prince Phillip was his cap.

"Maleficent!" they all said at the same time.

"She's got Prince Phillip!" Merryweather cried.

"At the Forbidden Mountains!" Flora added.

Fauna's eyes widened in horror. "But we can't go there!"

In spite of their magic powers, the fairies had never dared venture into Maleficent's domain.

"We *can*," Flora said firmly, "and we *must*!"

Without another word, the fairies were off. They raced out of the cottage and into the darkness of the Forbidden Mountains. The jagged spires of Maleficent's decaying castle loomed closer.

The fairies quickly flew past the crumbling stone bridges and the horrid winged gargoyles. A chilly wind pitched them right and left as they flew in and out of broken remnants of the castle walls.

The fairies could hear loud screeches coming from one wing of the castle. They flew toward the noise at once. Hiding on a deep window ledge, their tiny faces flickered with red and orange as they watched a crackling bonfire in the room below. Maleficent's creatures danced wildly around the fire, screaming so loudly that the fairies had to cover their ears.

Watching the bonfire coolly from her throne, Maleficent smiled. "What a pity Prince Phillip can't be here to enjoy the cel-

ebration," she said. She turned to her raven, who sat contentedly
on her shoulder. "Come. We must go to the dungeon and cheer
him up."

She rose from the throne and walked out of the room, carrying
her staff. The fairies fluttered silently behind, following her and
the raven through a long cavernous hallway and down a steep,
drafty stairwell. At the bottom, Maleficent pushed open a heavy
wooden door.

Inside was the slumped figure of Prince Phillip. He sat on a bench across the room, his wrists and ankles shackled to the wall with chains.

"Oh, come now, Prince Phillip," Maleficent said as a wicked smile crossed her lips. "Why so melancholy? A wondrous future lies before you."

She tipped her staff toward him. Its crystal ball began to glow

with an image of Aurora, motionless on her bed. "Behold King Stefan's castle!" Maleficent said. "And in yonder topmost tower, dreaming of her true love, is the princess Aurora!"

Prince Phillip gasped.

"Surprised?" Maleficent taunted. "Yes, it is the same peasant maid who won the heart of our noble prince just yesterday. But have no fear. I shall let you go . . . someday. The gates of the dungeon shall part, and you will ride valiantly away to awaken your love with true love's kiss."

The image changed. Now the crystal ball showed the prince as a stooped, white-haired old man, entering the castle grounds on a limping horse.

Prince Phillip gritted his teeth. He pulled at his chains violently, but they held fast.

Maleficent only laughed. "Come, my pet," she said to her raven. "Let us leave our noble prince with these happy thoughts."

The fairies flew into a crack in the wall as Maleficent walked out the door. "A most gratifying day," the witch purred, slamming the dungeon door behind her. "For the first time in sixteen years, I shall sleep well."

When Maleficent was gone, the fairies flew out of the crack. Waving their wands, they returned to normal size.

Prince Phillip looked up with a start. "Who—"

"Shhh!" Flora insisted. "No time to explain!" With a stroke of their magic wands, she and Fauna destroyed his chains, and Merryweather did the same to the lock on the door.

Finally free, Prince Phillip hopped to his feet. His eyes burned with vengeance as he bolted for the door.

"Wait, Prince Phillip!" Flora warned. As he turned to her, she waved her wand again. "The road to true love may be barred by many dangers, so arm thyself with these."

In a shower of crystal light, a glittering sword and shield appeared in Prince Phillip's hands. "Take this enchanted Shield of Virtue and this mighty Sword of Truth," Flora continued, "for these weapons of righteousness will triumph over evil!"

Prince Phillip took firm hold of the weapons. With grim determination, he led the fairies upstairs. But when they reached the top, a loud squawk pierced the air. The raven, who had been standing guard, now flew quickly toward the throne room.

There was little time left. The prince and the fairies raced blindly through a maze of dark archways and winding corridors.

Before long, there was a clamor of footsteps and shouting behind them. The fairies quickly shrunk themselves down again. His heart racing, the prince rounded a corner at top speed.

"Arrrghhh!" came an inhuman cry as a team of Maleficent's goons ambushed him.

The prince unsheathed his sword. Single-handedly he fought the creatures, and the corridor echoed with the clanking of metal against metal. Out of the corner of his eye, Prince Phillip spotted a window high above him. With a mighty thrust, he drove the creatures back, then leapt up onto the ledge.

The evening mist curled around his face. He couldn't see down to the ground, but he did see another long, broken ledge that led away from the window.

It was Phillip's only chance for escape. He stepped out onto the ledge. In the shifting fog, he saw a turret to his left. Inside it,

he could see Maleficent's guards frantically aiming their bows and arrows at him.

Below him, he heard Samson whinny. There was no time to think. He jumped.

The prince landed on a mound of earth. He slid down to the bottom and found himself in a courtyard of broken stone. Samson stood shackled to the wall a few feet away.

"Phillip, watch out!" came Flora's voice.

Prince Phillip's eyes shot upward. Maleficent's warriors lined the castle walls. With a rumble that shook the ground, heavy black boulders were being hurled toward him. Even his shield wouldn't protect him from those.

Flora waved her magic wand, sending fairy dust toward the rocks. *Zzzing!* They instantly changed into delicate bubbles that floated harmlessly away.

Merryweather shot fairy dust at Samson's shackles, breaking them to pieces. Prince Phillip hopped on his saddle, and Samson sped across the courtyard.

The creatures were screaming with anger. From the turret they now shot a barrage of arrows at the prince, and from directly overhead they poured out a vat of boiling oil.

But the fairies were ready. *Zzzing! Zzzing!* The arrows became lovely flowers, and the oil changed into an arched rainbow. Phillip galloped right underneath it at full speed.

A small shadow streaked over Merryweather's head. She looked up to see the raven. "You . . . ," she muttered angrily. Clutching her wand, she began to chase him.

The raven dodged in and out of the castle's spires and gargoyles. Merryweather shot fairy dust at the bird again and again but missed each time. Finally, as he flew behind a tower, she sim-

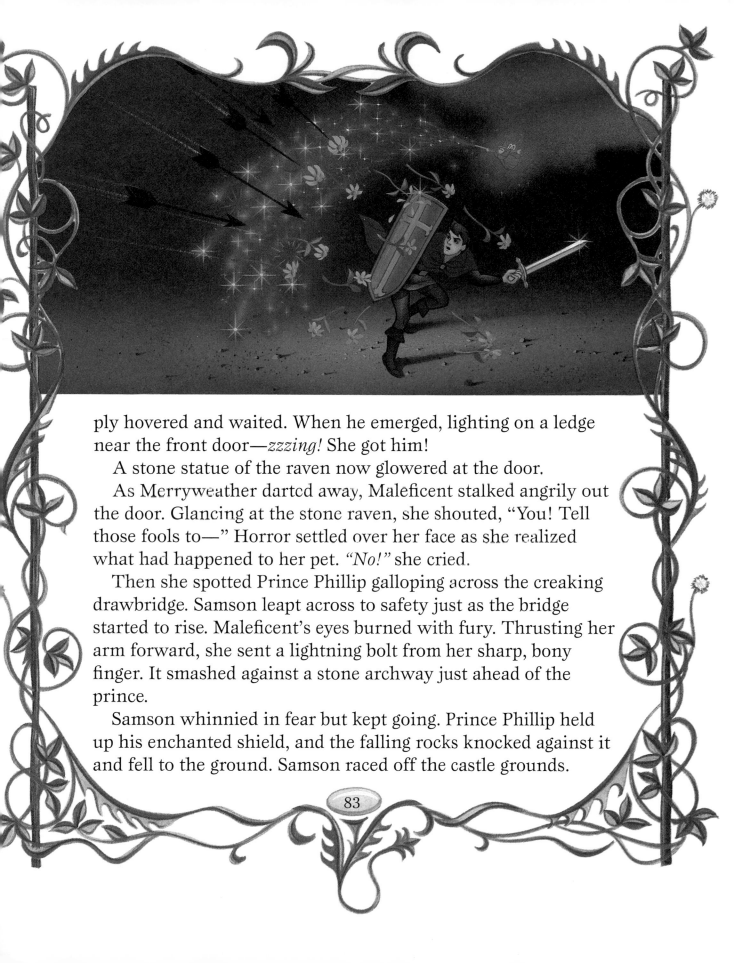

ply hovered and waited. When he emerged, lighting on a ledge near the front door—*zzzing!* She got him!

A stone statue of the raven now glowered at the door.

As Merryweather darted away, Maleficent stalked angrily out the door. Glancing at the stone raven, she shouted, "You! Tell those fools to—" Horror settled over her face as she realized what had happened to her pet. *"No!"* she cried.

Then she spotted Prince Phillip galloping across the creaking drawbridge. Samson leapt across to safety just as the bridge started to rise. Maleficent's eyes burned with fury. Thrusting her arm forward, she sent a lightning bolt from her sharp, bony finger. It smashed against a stone archway just ahead of the prince.

Samson whinnied in fear but kept going. Prince Phillip held up his enchanted shield, and the falling rocks knocked against it and fell to the ground. Samson raced off the castle grounds.

Ahead of him was a crevice in the earth just narrow enough to leap over. . . .

CRRRRAACCCCK! Maleficent hurled another bolt. It hit the crevice, opening it too wide to cross. Horse and rider slid downward on a steep pile of rocks and dirt. Samson struggled to keep upright. He hit the bottom on all fours and, leaping up the ravine with all his strength, made it to the other side.

The fairies followed him, three specks of bright light.

Maleficent watched, her rage boiling inside her. If the prince wanted a fight, she was ready for him. She raised her staff high and chanted,

A forest of thorns shall be his tomb,
Borne to the skies on a fog of doom.
Now go with a curse and serve me well.
Round Stefan's castle cast my spell!

Prince Phillip dug his heels into Samson's flanks. He could see King Stefan's castle in the distance. There were only a few miles left. . . .

CRRRRAACCCCK! Maleficent's lightning coated the countryside in blinding whiteness. For a moment, Prince Phillip could see nothing. He shielded his eyes and pulled back on Samson's reins.

When his eyes recovered, he no longer saw the castle. A black forest of thorny vines now blocked his view. The vines were rising upward at an uncanny speed, twining around each other, choking off all light. They hardened and thickened, and the thorns became as sharp as daggers.

No ordinary sword could possibly cut these vines. But Prince

Phillip's blade glowed with the magic of the fairies. He rode forward at full speed, swinging with all his might.

Whack! His sword sliced cleanly through a vine. It fell to the ground with a heavy thump.

Whack! Whack! Whack! Vine after vine tumbled away. With each thrust, the prince fought his way ever closer to the castle.

Far behind him, Maleficent stared in disbelief. "It cannot be!" she said.

In a fiery whirl, the witch rose into the air. She hurtled herself across the countryside, landing in front of Prince Phillip in a blazing ball of fire.

Samson reared up at the flames. The prince struggled to keep him steady.

"Now you shall deal with me, O Prince," Maleficent thundered, "and all the powers of *evil*!"

She disappeared into the ball of fire, which began to swell. The prince drew back his sword. The fairies looked on, terrified at whatever might happen next.

BOOOOMMMMM! An explosion shook the ground, and the ball of fire seemed to swallow everything around it, as if Maleficent had suddenly brought the sun to the earth.

Then, in the midst of the jumping flames, Maleficent's figure shot upward and transformed into a huge dragon. Its head loomed higher than the highest tree, and its eyes were a fiery orange. Its deep violet scales glinted like armor. Each time it breathed, its mouth spewed a roaring column of fire. The heat of its breath knocked Prince Phillip off Samson, who galloped away in terror.

HHHHHAAAAAA! A fiery blast shot toward the prince. He scrambled behind a thicket of vines.

By the silence that followed, he could tell the dragon had lost sight of him. He waited, watching the shadow of the dragon's head coming closer . . . closer . . .

At the last moment the prince jumped out of hiding. With a solid *whack*, he struck the dragon over the head.

The sword bounced off. Bellowing with anger and pain, the dragon blew fire over the entire forest. Flames rose from the ground, surrounding Prince Phillip on all sides.

"Up!" came Flora's voice from above. "Up this way!"

Phillip looked around to see his only path of escape—up a smooth cliff untouched by the flames. Digging in with his fingers, he scrambled to the top.

The prince barely had time to get to his feet before the dragon materialized before him. Now it, too, stood on the cliff.

Prince Phillip was trapped. If he moved backward, he would fall over the cliff into a bed of flames.

The dragon lunged toward him. It opened its mouth to draw a breath. Prince Phillip raised his magic shield.

HHHHHAAAAA! The flame hit the shield like the volley of a cannon. The shield flew out of the prince's hands and over the cliff.

He held up his sword, but it was of little use. The heat was now too great for him to get close to the dragon. In desperation, he drew back his arm and took aim at the dragon's head.

Above him, the fairies hovered anxiously. Together they sent a flurry of magic dust toward his sword.

Flora quickly chanted, "Sword of Truth fly swift and sure, that Evil die and Good endure!"

Phillip threw the sword, and it sliced through the air, its point gleaming with the good magic of the fairies. For a moment, it seemed to disappear into the flames.

But the anguished screech of the dragon left no doubt where
the sword had landed. Staggering forward, the dragon opened its
huge mouth. The sword was buried deep in its heart. It bared its
teeth and lurched toward the prince, ready to swallow him whole.

Prince Phillip ducked away. The giant jaws snapped shut
inches from his face. The dragon, weakened with pain, could not
stop itself from falling forward.

With a bellow that seemed to blot out all other sounds on
earth, the dragon plunged over the cliff to its fiery death.

The prince looked over the edge. He could see the shank of his
sword among the smoldering flames. Impaled on the sword was a
black cape. It was all that remained of Maleficent.

CHAPTER TEN

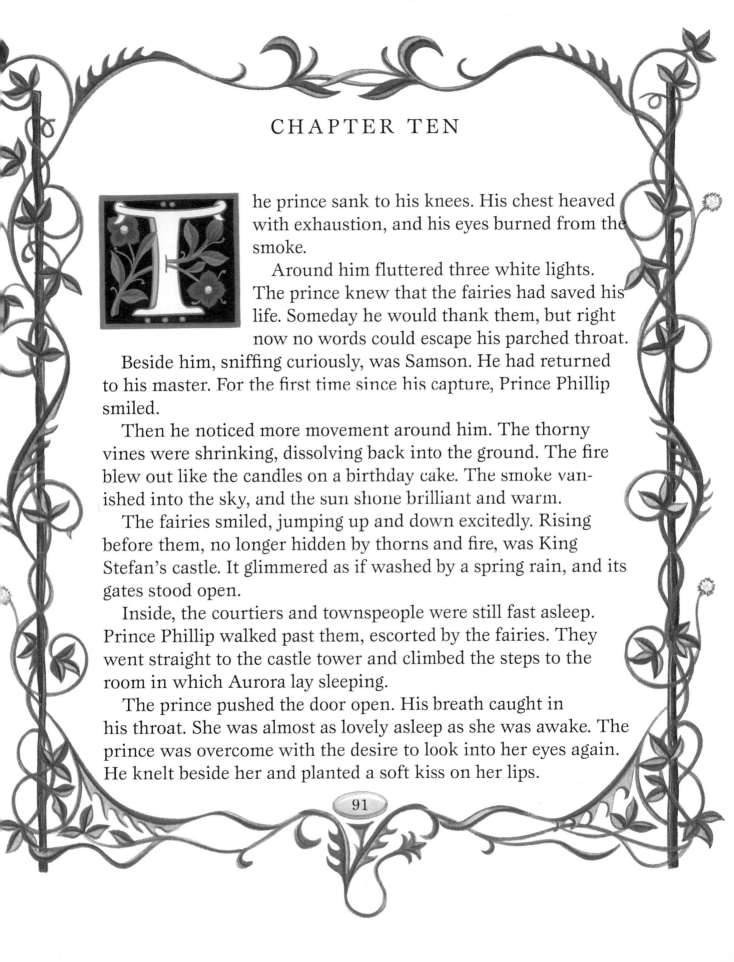

he prince sank to his knees. His chest heaved with exhaustion, and his eyes burned from the smoke.

Around him fluttered three white lights. The prince knew that the fairies had saved his life. Someday he would thank them, but right now no words could escape his parched throat.

Beside him, sniffing curiously, was Samson. He had returned to his master. For the first time since his capture, Prince Phillip smiled.

Then he noticed more movement around him. The thorny vines were shrinking, dissolving back into the ground. The fire blew out like the candles on a birthday cake. The smoke vanished into the sky, and the sun shone brilliant and warm.

The fairies smiled, jumping up and down excitedly. Rising before them, no longer hidden by thorns and fire, was King Stefan's castle. It glimmered as if washed by a spring rain, and its gates stood open.

Inside, the courtiers and townspeople were still fast asleep. Prince Phillip walked past them, escorted by the fairies. They went straight to the castle tower and climbed the steps to the room in which Aurora lay sleeping.

The prince pushed the door open. His breath caught in his throat. She was almost as lovely asleep as she was awake. The prince was overcome with the desire to look into her eyes again. He knelt beside her and planted a soft kiss on her lips.

The fairies held their breath.

Slowly Aurora's eyes flickered once, then twice. When they caught sight of Prince Phillip, they opened fully. Then a warm smile brought the princess's face back to life.

Bursting with happiness, the fairies squealed and hugged each other. "Come, you two!" Flora said happily to the couple. "To the royal court!"

All over the castle, people began to stir. Arms stretched, and mouths yawned.

In the throne room, a groggy King Stefan picked up his head. "Oh . . . forgive me," he said to King Hubert, who was yawning beside him. "You were saying . . . something about Phillip?"

"Huh?" King Hubert mumbled. "Oh, yes! Well, to come to the point, my son Phillip says he's going to marry a—"

The blare of a trumpet fanfare cut him off. All eyes focused on the top of the grand stairway. Prince Phillip and Princess Aurora appeared arm in arm, beaming with a joy that lit up the room.

King Stefan rose to his feet. His heart filled with happiness. His daughter was alive and well—and more beautiful than he could have imagined. "It's Aurora!" he cried.

King Hubert rubbed his eyes. "And . . . and . . . *Phillip*?"

The young couple approached the throne. Queen Leah's eyes brimmed with tears of relief. The years of worry seemed to rise from deep within her and fly away.

When Aurora got close to the queen, she could restrain herself no longer. She ran into Leah's arms. And she received an embrace that poured sixteen years of a mother's love into her heart.

Around them, the courtiers and townspeople burst into applause. It was the happiest day any of them had ever known.

The couple hugged and kissed King Stefan, then King Hubert.

"What . . . what does this mean, boy?" King Hubert asked his son, still confused.

But the court musicians had struck up a dance, and Prince Phillip whisked the princess away to the dance floor.

"I don't understand," King Hubert muttered. Then, with a sigh, he shrugged his shoulders and swayed to the music.

From a balcony high above, the fairies watched the prince and the princess dance. Fauna sobbed uncontrollably.

"Why, what's the matter, dear?" Flora asked.

Fauna sniffed. "Oh, I just love happy endings."

"Yes, I do, too," Flora said. She turned contentedly to see Aurora swirling gracefully, her dress a whirl of sky blue. *"Blue?"* she blurted, her contentment disappearing.

Zzzing! She waved her wand and turned it pink.

Now Merryweather's smile disappeared. *"Blue!"* she demanded. *Zzzing!* went her wand.

On the dance floor, Aurora looked lovingly into the eyes of her prince. Her dress flashed pink and blue in a swirl of motion. But to her and everyone around her, it was just another magical part of this most magical dream come true.